Sometimes Love Ain't

ENOUGH

SOMETIMES LOVE AIN'T ENOUGH

J.L. MINYARD

CENTURION
BOOKS

First Edition. July 2022
Published by Centurion Books

www.jessicaminyard.com

ISBN: 978-1-957004-02-0
eBook ISBN: 978-1-957004-03-7
Cover by Qamber Designs & Media

This book contains material that may be sensitive to some readers.

For Alex—who wrote me poetry

CHAPTER ONE

HEART EYES

I find it horribly ironic that my mom named her fat kid after one of the thinnest actors in American cinema. Mom probably couldn't have guessed I'd grow up to be fat, but she sure as hell should have known the pressure of a sleek twenty-five-inch waist was going to be too much for a girl to handle.

My index finger hovered ominously above the Backspace key. Even now, when the woman was over two hundred miles away and would never even see what I wrote, I hesitated. The cursor blinked, taunting.

"Dammit."

I saved my dismal progress and clicked away from the Word document and dived into my school email account instead.

"What's wrong?" my roommate, Amera, asked from the couch, where she was idly downing ramen noodles and watching reruns of *Law & Order: Special Victims Unit*.

"This fucking personal statement is proving to be rather difficult."

"How so? Thought you liked talking about yourself."

"Har har har. Bite me."

But we both knew it was true.

I didn't normally have such a hard time putting words to paper, especially when the topic was myself. I was a burgeoning journalist, after all, and had my own advice column in the *Penn Warren University Ledger*, which I had lucked into freshman year. It was originally only supposed to be a life and general college advice column, but then I started getting dating and relationship help emails, and, well, there's not much more scintillating to college students than anonymous emails about basketball players and hot TAs. Thus, my dating advice column was born.

I would also sometimes answer questions live on the university's radio station, so being speechless was not really an issue of mine. I liked to talk about everything.

But what if my mom—magically, inexplicably—got her hands on my essay? And God forbid, *read* it. What would she think?

I snorted with contempt. I would worry about deconstructing all of that emotional baggage later. I still had like three months before the application was due and the only thing missing was the personal statement. I had time.

"You bastard!" Amera shouted at the TV. I didn't know how she could stay so engrossed on the fifth or sixth go around with the series. I had my own comfort shows as well, but I usually turned them on for background noise, not watch them through every time like it was the first time. She stabbed her fork at the TV. "It's always the guest star."

Odafin, our shared one-eye rescue cat, had skittered under the safety of the desk after Amera's outburst and was rubbing his orange self all up on my black leggings. I rubbed him with a toe. Neither of us were really cat people, but Odafin and the house seemed to come as a package deal. We found him lurking around outside when we moved in, mangy and mewling every night at the front windows.

Eventually, we broke, left out a can of tuna, and then, as they say, the rest was history.

I glanced back at my email, Odafin vibrating against my leg. I had a few questions for my column, appropriately named The Wrong Swipe. It used to be just Ask Bryn, but I had successfully petitioned to rename and rebrand when it blew up.

Dear Bryn,

I caught my boyfriend cheating with one of my sorority sisters. He says he's sorry but I'm finding it hard to forgive him. We're high school sweethearts and he gave me a promise ring senior year. What do I do?????

Ditch his cheating loser ass, obviously.

There. All done.

Of course, I'd have to go back and flesh out my response a little bit. My editor liked all my answers to be at least a couple hundred words, as to fill out my allotted space before local ads kicked in.

I attempted to outline the rest of my answer without going on a long rant about promise rings but kept getting distracted by the joyous way Amera was slurping her noodles. One of the downfalls of our shared desk being in the living room. I hadn't had anything to eat today except a protein shake and a granola-topped yogurt almost nine hours ago and I was probably dying.

Amera was, in a word, statuesque. An effortlessly statuesque girl who could eat five cheeseburgers—and would eat five cheeseburgers—and never gain a pound or an inch. I'd hate her and her mile-high legs if I didn't already love her.

I snapped the rubber band on my wrist.

Another one of my mother's ideas that she'd gleaned from a celebrity or self-appointed diet guru. A little pain response association to teach me to fear the food, I guess.

Amera's head swiveled towards me, cutting her off midslurp.

"What did you just do?"

I held up my wrist. "Mom's suggestion."

Her dark eyes narrowed.

One of the many reasons I loved her. She didn't police her own body, and refused to let me police mine, at least while she was watching. Well, I policed it a little, but not to the extent my mom would like.

Amera and I met during a dorm floor meeting freshman year. We bonded over her Star Wars shirt, our favorite Reylo fanfics, and my Cardan quote tattoo. We were trash for dramatic sad boys.

She came home with me over Thanksgiving break that year. My mom always made an elaborate six-course meal, half of which I wasn't supposed to indulge in. Everything was going swimmingly, until my mom looked at Amera and asked her if she thought she'd had enough stuffing, because she had such a *lovely* figure to maintain.

The way my mom had looked at Amera and the way "such" had dripped from her mouth had made my stomach turn. The envy and admiration and jealousy were palpable.

Fork halfway to mouth, Amera had stopped, grinned, showing all her teeth, and proceeded to devour the rest of the stuffing as my mom watched, open-mouthed with horror.

No one had ever stood up to my mother like that. Even me. Especially not me.

Amera's defiance had made me bold enough to finish all the food on my plate, when I would have otherwise picked around it to show my mom how in control of myself I was. That stunt had earned me a month's worth of concerned texts and emailed weight loss articles.

Sophomore year I went to Amera's house for Thanksgiving and it was so wonderful to be able to sit and eat a meal without judgement that I'd cried over my sweet potatoes and stuffing. Made a great first impression on the Rees family.

"Fine." I sighed.

Under her glare, I slipped the rubber band off and threw it on top of the pile of rubble I was accumulating on our desk.

Suddenly, there was a flurry of pounding on the front door. Odafin bolted for the safety of the back bedrooms.

"Open the door, minions!"

Ah, Sebastian Rees, Amera's twin, had arrived.

Sebastian still lived in the dorms but was at our house often enough that we always kept a stack of clean blankets and pillows handy so that he could crash on the couch. Amera still hadn't been able to convince him to pay rent, though.

Amera let him in with an eye roll, and I greeted him enthusiastically.

"Bastian!"

He held up a 12-pack of White Claw and a plastic bag. "Happy Birthday, love."

Ah, yes, today happened to be my twenty-first birthday. My Facebook notifications had been going off all day. I had yet to hear anything from my mother, but my best friend from high school had sent me a bouquet of twenty-one roses.

I got up and wrapped my arms around Bastian's lean middle. "You smell delicious."

"I know." He kissed the top of my head. Bastian was wearing tight joggers, high-top Jordans, and a long tank top that was slit up both sides to reveal a dark and taut abdomen. Unlike Amera, Bastian did put in the work, and had the sculpted arms and tight abs to prove it.

I pulled away. "Wait a minute. Are you glittering?"

He grinned. "I brought enough for everyone." He set the Claw down on the coffee table and pulled out a jar of gold glitter and a makeup brush from the plastic bag.

Amera grabbed the jar and inspected it. "Why do you always have to be so extra?"

"It's Bryn's *twenty-first* birthday." He also pulled out a sash and tiara. "Are we going to start getting ready or what?"

I glanced at my phone for the first time. Only 7:30 p.m. But we needed to get started if we were going to get out of the house anywhere close to nine.

Sebastian was already mostly ready, so he could relax on the couch with Odafin and judge our outfits as we paraded from bedrooms to living room.

The house was a small two-bedroom, two-bath, one-floor ranch that was rented out to Penn Warren students by an old alumni couple. Since Amera's parents were our connection, she got the owner's suite and paid a smidge more in rent. Her parents had also provided most of our living room furniture, which was mostly overstuffed and too big for the space. We didn't mind because it was all great for naps.

I honestly hated going dancing when it was hot out. But I had been cursed with a May birthday and there wasn't shit-else to do when drinking and celebrating in a college town that basically shut down over summer break, when everyone went home.

It was so hard to get unsweaty when you couldn't step outside for cool air. But I wasn't exactly trolling for dudes tonight, so I would probably be okay.

Amera poked her head into my bedroom.

"Are you gonna pick already? We have to do faces!"

Amera was already dressed. She'd chosen a pair of high and tight black shorts, a strapless gold top, dangly gold earrings, and sensible cork wedges. Half of her braids had been tied on top of her head.

I felt a stab of jealousy at how easy it was for her to just pull clothes out and put them on without having to worry about how and where they'd stick and pull; how they would look damp and sweaty. Which ones would look *less* damp and sweaty. Amera would be sweaty at the end of the night too. That was just a reality when you go drinking and dancing at the end of May in the sticky Southern heat. But sweaty fat girls and sweaty slender girls were not the same.

I eyed the pile of discarded clothes on my bed. "Yeah, almost done."

She disappeared and I heard her yelling at Bastian for drinking the last mango White Claw.

In the end I chose a tank dress with a tight bodice and swishy skirt. It was black, and I added a thin black belt under the bust to emphasize my most impressive features. I put on silver hoops and pulled my dyed green hair up into a tight bun, to make room for the birthday tiara.

I grabbed my bags of makeup and half-drunk Claw on my way to the kitchen, where Sebastian was already working on Amera's eyes.

"Oh, me next!"

I dropped my bags on the table next to Amera's. She glanced my way—well, as much as she could with Bastian holding her chin. "Girl, damn. No one's going to be looking at your face."

"Thanks." I faux curtsied before taking a seat.

I started my foundation and highlighter process while I waited for Bastian to finish Amera's wings. After eyeliner, it was on to false eyelashes, which were infinitely easier to put on with assistance. I could do them myself, but I usually ended up with space between lash and skin and glue all over my finger nails.

Bastian's phone beeped. "Five minutes till the Uber is here!"

We finished spritzing and dabbing and applying Bastian's fancy gold body glitter. The room was heavy with three very distinct smells: spicy cedar and ginger for Bastian, coconut for Amera, and white gardenia and jasmine for me. Together we were an odiferous bouquet.

"I need pictures!"

I grabbed them both and we made our usual triangle. Being the shortest, I was always in the front, but Bastian held the phone. We took a few photos with the sash, and a few photos without the sash, and proceeded to take pictures until Bastian's phone went off again.

"Uber is here!"

"Who's got a key?"

Amera swung her bright red messenger bag over her shoulder. "Got it."

I grabbed a tiny black clutch which only fit my ID, lipstick, cash, and maybe phone if I squeezed it in there real tight.

Bastian was already out the door and bouncing down the front steps to a green Camry, which must have been our ride.

Amera grabbed my hand. "Let's go, birthday girl."

I spent the ride over filtering and posting the best pictures to Instagram and my stories, tagging Bastian. Amera wasn't on any social media platforms, much to my dismay and suspicion when we first started hanging out. I thought she must be either a serial killer or in the witness protection program. It was so odd to meet someone who had literally no online presence whatsoever, save for a few mentions in old sports articles from high school.

Amera had explained it as just not caring at all what other people thought of her life, real or imaginary, and that anyone she really liked or cared about could text her. Touché. Not that it stopped her from helping me cultivate my Instagram image or scrolling through my Tinder when I wasn't watching.

I'd found many a message from interested dudes that I wouldn't have necessarily chosen for myself. Amera had a type, and he wasn't my type, usually.

The club Bastian had scoped out—452—was new to our area, and nestled on a busy street with other restaurants and retail businesses. The addition of 452 brought the number of bars in our area up to a grand total of three. One had a reputation for being sleezy and the other hosted too many karaoke nights for the average college kid to be interested. 452 had been the shiny new attraction all spring semester.

Our Uber driver stopped right in front of the door—452 in bright neon overhead—so we had to hustle to get out of his car before other drivers got upset and the honking started.

There was a burly, bearded bouncer guarding the door, stamping the backs of people's hands.

He smiled at me and Amera. "Have a good night, ladies."

His eyes lingered on my exposed bosom and his fingers lingered on mine as he stamped 452 on my hand.

Amera glanced back as we entered the club, blasted immediately by blessedly cold air. "He was interested."

I looped my arm through hers. Bastian had already disappeared into the crowd. "I'm just here to have a good time with my friends. No hookups."

Amera looked skeptical. "If you say so."

I poked her in the ribs. "It's true!"

"You said that last weekend."

Okay, maybe she had a point. I filed away the bouncer's lusty gaze just in case I changed my mind by the end of the night.

452 was moderately crowded for the summer break. The tiny outside façade was deceptive; the inside of the club was pleasantly sprawling with a stage and a long bar. There was a live band currently on stage, crooning country song covers, every member wearing boots and cowboy hats. The lead singer was pretty cute, so there was a gaggle of thin-hipped white girls dancing up front with much enthusiasm but very little rhythm.

"I need a drink," Amera said.

"Me too."

At the bar, the guy who'd been buying me drinks all night had his hand planted firmly on my ass. Three drinks ago, it'd been at the small of my back.

He leaned in and whispered, "Same thing? Or do you want to try something harder?"

He pressed up against me, meaning abundantly, obnoxiously clear.

I giggled and batted my fake eyelashes, as was expected.

In the dim bar, I couldn't really tell if he was all that cute or if I was just that drunk. He had a mess of shaggy hair and a scratchy beard, but that's about all I could recall.

Before anything else could be said or implied, I felt my phone start vibrating in quick succession.

I held a finger up to his mouth. "Hold that thought."

I fished out my phone and thumbed in the code and my stomach roiled and it had nothing to do with the vodka and ginger ale I'd been drinking. I swayed ominously, which only made Shaggy Hair Random Guy clutch at me tighter.

I glanced at the dance floor where Amera was tangled up with a tall, lanky white boy I recognized from sophomore biology. Couldn't remember his name, though. They were looking *very* cozy, his fingers skimming the exposed skin of her thighs.

"Amera!" I all but squealed in her direction.

Her head whipped around and something in my face must have communicated the urgency of the situation because she extracted herself right quick and headed my way.

"What's up?"

I shoved my phone up under her nose and hissed, "Look at this."

Shaggy Hair Random Guy also happened to be looking over my shoulder as well.

He snorted. "Really?"

"Yeah, go away." That sounded harsh. "Sorry."

His mouth turned up in a nasty scowl, but at least he walked away without a fight. I had an emergency and couldn't deal with some dickhead being upset about a few free drinks.

Amera grabbed my phone hand to steady it. "Stop moving." She poked through my notifications, a deep line forming in the middle of her perfectly sculpted brows.

I had three new Instagram notifications from *him*. He'd reacted to my story, and left two comments on my most recent picture.

Damn. Followed by three fire emojis and one heart eyes.

"Wait," I said. "There's more."

I opened up my text messages and the most recent one was left unopened at the top.

Happy birthday, baby girl <3

She side-eyed me. "Are you going to answer?"

I stared at the text message, vision blurring and face heating. "I don't know. Should I?"

"No, but you're not going to listen to me, are you?"

"Yes. Yes, I am."

I pushed the power button to shut the screen down and was about to slip it back into my tiny purse and go find Shaggy Hair

Random Guy but that's when it started the steady buzz of an incoming call.

Justin Hershaw, or just Shaw, as he was basically called by literally everyone else in our hometown, was hitting up my phone again.

Shaw had been somewhat of my high school sweetheart, sorta. I lost my virginity to him at prom when I was fifteen, but I hadn't been his date. Or his girlfriend. After that night, I still wasn't his girlfriend. We were a secret that was all ours—secret and special. Sure, he might have officially dated other girls, but he always came back to me.

It had been about six months since I'd heard from him, but that was how things went with us. He'd ghost, I'd be too proud to reach out first, he'd pop back up, and I wouldn't be too proud to pick up.

One night, I'd drunkenly relayed the whole sordid story to Amera, probably more than I'd told anyone else. Her opinion of him had immediately soured, but she didn't know him. Hadn't even met him.

I let the first call go to voicemail, clutching the phone so tight my knuckles were turning white. I let out a breath, some of the tension leaving my body.

A second call came in.

I couldn't look at her anymore.

"I'll be right back."

I made a beeline for the front door, smiling at the bouncer and telling him I'd be right back.

Walking a little bit down the sidewalk, I found a relatively quiet and empty expanse of wall and leaned back, bracing myself. Steadying my voice.

"Hello?"

"Hey." His deep, husky voice melted into my ear from the other end of the phone.

"Oh, hey, Justin." Yes, cool, calm, and collected like a little cucumber.

"Didn't forget about me, did ya?" He laughed, and it was silky velvet. I definitely shouldn't have had so many vodka ginger ales.

I laughed back. "Of course not."

"Haven't heard from you in a while."

Uh, yeah, same, dude. But instead, "I've been busy with school and work and the usual. I've got a lot going on." I resisted the urge to apologize.

"Yeah, I can see that." I knew he could see that because we followed each other on Instagram. I knew he would like the black dress, the expanse of skin it showed, the sultry makeup. Like a fish to a lure. "Hey, are you seeing anybody?"

And now we'd reached the point of the phone call. I thought about Shaggy Hair Random Guy. "Not anyone serious. What about you?" I resisted the urge to sound so concerned. I mimed examining my fingernails to keep my voice light.

"Nah, I ditched Bekah a while ago. I think she was runnin' around on me, man. I can't really count on anyone these days, ya know. Except you."

There it was.

I could feel my face flush with pleasure, as it always did when he acknowledged the truth about us, about me.

"Hey, I want to see you soon. Can I drive up?"

I started. "What? You have a ride?"

Shaw was always between cars, between jobs, between beds. I'd been at Penn Warren going on four years and he'd never been able to come up and see me. I always had to go home.

That laugh again. "Yeah, got a new set of wheels. Text me back, okay? Miss you, baby girl."

And then he was gone.

I sagged against the wall, ignoring the brick digging into my skin, a bubble of happiness expanding within my chest.

Footsteps were approaching while I stared at my phone, smiling. My first thought was that it was Amera or Bastian coming to find me and return me to my senses. But a pair of leather sneakers inched into my vision and neither of the Rees twins would wear such shoes.

"Hey."

Oh, great. It was Shaggy Hair Random Guy, come to find me again. Dude was clingy. We hadn't even grinded that much on the dance floor for this level of commitment.

"Everything okay?"

I finally looked up, annoyed. He was interrupting my train of thought and I was trying to think up the perfect response to Shaw's most recent text. Not too eager. Aloof and mysterious.

"Yeah, I'm good."

"Do you want to go back in?" He nodded towards the door.

"No, I'm going to chill out here for a bit. Thanks for the drinks, though."

Turned out he was kind of cute, in an average, every day, suburban husband kind of way. His cute face fell, just a little bit. "Oh, well, happy birthday, then."

He shuffled his feet, hands in the pockets of his jeans, and just stood there.

Oh, God, he wasn't leaving. Was this dude not going to take no for an answer? Was I going to have to make a scene?

"Hey, my man, I'm trying to hook back up with my ex, so could you like, just leave me to it?"

Leave me to self-destruct in peace and silence, please, kay, thanks.

His eyes widened. I'm sure he'd never had a potential one-night date give him the truth like that before.

"Yeah, okay, good luck with that."

I gave him a thumbs-up as he finally walked away.

CHAPTER TWO

NIGHT OF THE REAPPEARING EXES

We made it back to the house sans Bastian, who'd found an old flame to go home with instead. Night of the Reappearing Exes, indeed.

Amera crawled into bed with a bottle of water and her purple silk bonnet—still in her party clothes.

I took the time to stop by my room and grab an old T-shirt and pajama pants, before tiptoeing back to Amera's room.

Amera's room was full of prints from obscure artists she found on the internet and vintage furniture and knickknacks. Her bed was pushed up against the wall, but she'd left enough room to climb in.

She'd left her makeup on too, so there was glitter and eyeliner smeared in the hollows under her eyes. She blinked at me blearily, contacts still in as well. She'd regret that in the morning, but it wouldn't be the first time.

"You should take your contacts out," I whispered.

"Is that really what you came in here to talk about," she said, in a voice raspy with alcohol and sleep. "Bryn. It's four in the morning. You better get it out before I pass out." Her lashes, heavy with the falsies, fluttered.

"Okay, so, Justin wants to come up to visit me." That got her attention and I powered on. "I just wanted to check with you and make sure it was okay if he stayed here. For, like, just a night."

She took a swig of her water, and I regretted the night I'd told her everything.

"He won't bring anything, will he? I can't have anything illegal in this house. I'm on a full scholarship, remember."

I vehemently shook my head. "He doesn't do that anymore."

At least, I didn't think he did. Shaw used to have a problem with pot and pills. While the marijuana wasn't a big deal—who hadn't smoked a little pot here and there—the pills were a different matter entirely. He always used to tell me he never did them; just bought and sold them to a small circle of friends, some of whom I had the unfortunate problem of meeting late at night at ramshackle houses and sometimes just in the middle of a deserted road when he needed a ride.

Her eyes narrowed suspiciously. "He better not. You know I'm not afraid to put a little white boy in his place."

I croaked out a laugh. "I know. I promise. Nothing like that. I'll even make dinner for us or something. It'll be nice."

She snorted. "Not if you're cooking."

I bumped her shoulder with mine. "That was unnecessary! I know how to cook exactly three dishes!"

"Stouffer's lasagna doesn't count as knowing how to cook a dish."

I pouted.

I could see her face grow serious in the moonlight creeping in between the cracked blinds.

"Are you sure you want to do this?" she asked solemnly. Like we were going to be hosting a funeral.

"Amera, it's not a big deal."

"That's not what I've heard."

I didn't know how to take back the things I'd said about Justin, or how to assuage her obvious concern about him now.

A cloud passed over the moon and plunged the room into darkness.

"This time will be different."

I could no longer see Amera's face, but I knew what expression she wore. One of skepticism and doubt.

This time will be different. I sent it out into the universe like a prayer. Manifest manifest manifest. If I thought about it hard enough, it would be so.

It had to be different this time.

Justin wanted to come up that weekend, so I only had to wait a few anxious days.

I had given him the address to our house and was waiting outside for him to pull up. During the summers and even into early fall, my usual uniform was dresses—of all shapes. I had picked my outfit today with great care: a floral maxi that was extremely flattering for my shape, hid some of my more problem areas (hello, cankles), and emphasized the better areas. There was a slit up one side to show a round thigh, and thin straps crisscrossed over my breasts.

I had even squeezed into a pair of shapewear shorts. I didn't usually wear shapewear, because fuck shapewear and trying to make my body appear smaller than it was, but it had been months since he'd seen me.

Not that I'd gotten any smaller in the interim.

Not that it really made much of a difference, but I felt better knowing that things were being held up high and tight and there wouldn't be any rogue jiggling.

My hair was up in a meticulously constructed messy bun and my makeup was carefully "natural."

Justin was late.

I inhaled a breath, trying to slow the rapid beating of my heart. And the rising panic. What if he didn't show?

That'd be a riot.

My phone buzzed. I almost flung it across the street in my haste to remove it from my small crossbody.

Five minutes.

I exhaled, deflating like an overstretched balloon. He was still coming.

A few minutes later, I saw a maroon PT Cruiser creeping up the narrow street. I resisted the urge to wave my arms frantically, er, excitedly.

I pretended to be engrossed in my phone instead, until he parked, exited, and stood right in front of me.

"Bored?"

Goddammit he was so fucking hot. Now I was too hot in the overhead May sun.

His steel-cut jaw boasted only a small amount of stubble, just enough to be felt rasping across your skin. His mouth was wide, bottom lip thicker than the top, but only barely. He wore a rugged pair of jeans and a plain T-shirt, floppy brown hair sweeping out the back of his backwards baseball cap.

Tendons strained and pulsed in his arms and neck; he was lean.

He was only maybe an inch taller than me, which always put his liquid brown eyes right on mine.

"Never," I said. And much to my surprise my voice managed to come out normal.

He smiled and it immediately transformed his face from intense and brooding to boyish and playful. Son of a bitch.

"Damn, girl, come here."

Without prompting, he grabbed my shoulders and pulled me tight to his chest. Or as tight as he could.

I tried to relax into the sensation, but it was hard to get lost in the warmth of his body when I was already uncomfortably warm everywhere else. Standing outside in the heat had caused the back of my neck and forehead to start sweating. My foundation was doing a hell of a job, though, bless it.

I wrapped my arms around his own angular waist and just tried to enjoy the contact.

"Nice digs," he said.

Our house was on a secluded corner lot, surrounded by mature trees that made the front porch a pleasant spot when the weather cooled down. The garden was a little overgrown—none of us did lawn care—but it was a cute place.

"Yeah, thanks. My roommate found it for us. Amera. You'll get to meet her later."

"Cool."

The hug ended and he took my sweaty palm instead. Fucking Christ, I needed to get in some air-conditioning immediately.

I tugged him towards the Cruiser and he took the hint, popping the lock.

We got in and the air was already blasting, thank God.

"So, what did you want to do? We have a couple hours before dinner." I'd given Amera money and she was going to pull something together that we'd be able to cook.

"Dinner, huh. Like something fancy?"

"Oh, no. Just something simple."

Justin didn't eat much, for whatever reason. Probably how he stayed so slim. I honestly don't know if I'd ever seen him eat a full meal, which meant I went hungry a lot too whenever we hung out. Because I sure as hell wasn't eating if he wasn't. I usually had to pick up food on my way home at ridiculous hours of the night or early morning.

Justin had pulled out his phone and was scrolling through screens. I resisted the urge to peek and see if I could see anything of interest. That never ended well for me because I usually caught him texting other girls or browsing the pages of lithe and bronzed Instagram models.

That's how I found out about Bekah the last time.

So I waited, watching the clouds scuttle by.

Finally, he said, "You know where Maple Street is?"

"Uh, yeah, I think so." Maple was a residential area, so not a place I would frequent. "What's there?"

He dropped his phone in the center console and put the car in drive. "A buddy. I need to swing by."

My stomach bottomed out. "Justin. You can't bring pills to our house."

He laughed. "I'm not. He's got some tools he's going to let me borrow. For a job."

The car swung out onto the main thoroughfare. The uneasy feeling lingered. Of course, he had never told me directly when we were going to score pills. It was always a different kind of errand. He needed to see a buddy. He needed to drop off something for a buddy. He needed to pick up something for a buddy.

Amera would literally murder me if we came back with pills.

Oh, and, hey, wasn't he here to see me?

"I thought we were going to hang out. You know, just us?" I hated the way my voice sounded. Hated the high-pitched upspeak that lingered at the end.

"Yeah, we are. It'll be quick."

It was not quick.

After we finally found his buddy's house, which was buried at the very end of Maple Street, we had to stay for a chitchat, apparently.

His buddy was a stout man who wore a stained shirt and his buddy's girlfriend looked especially hard-worn and aggrieved. Mascara was smeared under her eyes and her acrylics were at least three weeks overgrown.

A cigarette dangled from her lipstick-stained mouth, and it took every ounce of self-control and mannered upbringing not to gag or grimace. The house reeked of cigarette smoke and cat poop.

"Shaw, your girl is hot," the buddy had drawled in greeting.

Oh, gross.

"Yeah, thanks," Justin said. And then he'd changed the subject.

I shot him a look. His girl? Is that what he had told these people? And what was that supposed to mean, exactly?

"Nice to meet you all," I said, with a small wave and what I hoped was a comfortable and friendly smile.

The house had all the shades drawn and it was stifling. The girlfriend offered me a drink, but I declined.

Then Justin and his buddy disappeared and left me in the living room with the girlfriend, who they hadn't really introduced me to so I didn't even know her name.

After a few horribly uncomfortable silent minutes, I finally broke.

"I'm sorry, I didn't catch your name."

"Mavis," she said.

"Oh, that's really pretty!"

And then silence descended once more.

Chapter Three

ACCIDENTAL THREESOME

Eventually, the boys came back to the living room, and Justin was actually carrying two black cases that looked like they could possibly contain power tools.

So maybe this visit wasn't as nefarious as I had first assumed. I still couldn't wait to leave, though.

Justin shook the other man's hand and said, "Thanks, man. I'll hit you up later."

"Sure, no problem." The man waved us out the door and I didn't need to be told twice. I practically leapt from the sagging recliner I'd been perched on.

Once outside, I shook out my dress, trying to dispel some of the cigarette smoke.

"I assume you got everything you needed?"

Justin put the cases in the back seat. "Yep." His voice sounded brighter, cheerier, than when he'd arrived.

I went to get back in the car, but instead of walking back to the driver's side door, Justin had walked around to mine and stood awfully close.

I slouched against the car door; it was an old trick to make myself shorter and therefore smaller and more desirable.

His eyes crinkled when he smiled. "Thanks for coming with me."

"Yeah, no problem. I didn't really do much."

He was leaning in closer, his chest pressing against my chest, the smile still lingering on his lips. He reeked of cigarettes, but, whatever. He slipped his arms around my waist, hands sliding to linger above the curve of my ass.

I put one hand on the side of his face, and he leaned into my touch, kissing my palm. My heartbeat stuttered at the warmth.

I slowly moved my hand lower, and his teeth snagged my thumb.

Jesus fucking Christ I was going to burst into flames in the gravel driveway of Mavis and Whatever His Name Was.

My hand landed on the veined column of his throat, where his pulse threaded, slow and steady. My own felt thunderous in comparison.

He finally finished the journey to my lips, and the kiss was chaste and leisurely. What the fuck. I resisted the urge to crush his body to mine, to ratchet up his desire, the way he was doing to mine with a close-mouthed smooch that was an insult to real kissing.

He pulled away and my hands caught in his shirt, almost as if they had a mind of their own.

"Easy, tiger, we don't want all the neighbors to see." That laugh again and I felt thoroughly chided, with a dash of embarrassment added for spice. Like we had been doing something wrong. Like I had, again, been caught wanting him more than he wanted me.

We both got into the car and I twisted my body to confront him as much as I could.

"Do you have a problem with kissing me where someone might see?"

He laughed like it was no big deal and that I was in the wrong to even think it was. The slit in my dress just happened to be on the left, and the full length of my thigh was exposed. Instead of reaching for the gear shift, his long-fingered hand found my thigh instead.

"I just want you all to myself, baby girl."

When we got back to the house, Bastian had already arrived with the wine, Amera was prepping a salad, and the oven was preheating for an easy chicken casserole.

My heart was in my throat. I couldn't control anything that was about to happen or anything that might be said. I trusted Amera not to say anything about the things I'd told her; she wouldn't do that to me.

"Uh, hey. Everyone, this is Justin."

His arm slid around my waist and I was bolstered by the contact.

He tipped his chin up in greeting. "'Sup."

"This is my roommate, Amera, and her twin, Sebastian."

Bastian popped the cork of a dark red Chianti. "What are you drinking?"

"Uh, you got any beer?"

Bastian grinned. "A man of discerning tastes, I see." He poured his own glass. "Yeah, we've got some Miller. I'll get you one. What you drinking, Brynnie?"

Justin's arm shifted and my stomach clenched. He didn't know about my nom de plume. And why would he? It wasn't something that really came up in casual conversation and he didn't go to my school. Didn't read the school newspaper and get to hear me correct every professor of every class on the first day.

What would he think about that?

Justin didn't say anything out loud, though. Just waited patiently for Bastian to return with his beer.

"Did you get any Moscato?" I said.

"You know I did."

Bastian poured me a glass of the sweet wine and handed Justin the beer.

Amera was giving me eyes as she sprinkled too much cheese into the salad. She was also following Justin's every move as he and Sebastian moved towards the living room. Like he was going to explode or get her expelled just by his sheer presence.

I sidled up next to her with my wine.

"He is hot, I'll give you that," she said begrudgingly.

I sipped my wine. "I know, right?"

"Short, though."

"What's wrong with short?"

Amera shrugged noncommittally. "Nothing. I've always found that short guys have thick dicks." Her eyes slid to me and gleamed.

"I will neither confirm nor deny that hypothesis." Taking another big gulp of wine, I made a gesture like I was guessing the measurement of a big fish.

Amera snorted. She tossed the salad with a wooden spoon with a little more intensity than I thought was completely necessary.

"Bastian seems to like him well enough. They found something to bond over."

They had managed to find a game of some sort on TV and were talking animatedly about college basketball, mostly over each other. I'm not sure they were actually talking to each other.

"He's not a bad guy," I said.

Amera pursed her lips, but decided not to comment. I'm sure she was remembering the choice words I had used to describe him previously: douche, dickhead, and asswipe had been among my favorites.

He wasn't a bad guy, though. He was charming, sweet, and smart when he tried. He had barely eked out a high school graduation, thanks in part to me for helping him pass senior English. So maybe he wasn't book smart and college bound. He was good with his hands and had a head for technical skills. He was the product of overly permissive parents who hadn't expected anything better from him. So, he'd lived up to those expectations, the bar set so low it might as well have been on the ground.

So what if he was a little flighty and had the attention span of a gnat. We were young; it didn't have to be serious for it to mean something.

Besides, he always came back to me, no matter what. I was the one who knew all his secrets and fears and hopes. Not those other fair-weather girls. They always left him and I wouldn't.

"Help me with this chicken, would ya."

Amera handed me a raw chicken breast.

I squealed. "Ack. What am I supposed to do with this?"

She pointed to a gooey mixture in a bowl on the counter. "Bread it. Obviously."

"That's going to get stuck under my nails."

She plopped a pale, slimy breast into the mixture. "For fuck's sake, stop being such a princess. Bread it!"

I held the chicken carefully between my thumb and forefinger. "This is why I only know how to cook frozen lasagna."

She laughed, deep and throaty, a laugh fated to draw attention. And it succeeded. Bastian and Justin looked our way; Bastian had a horrified expression on his face.

"Amera, no! Are you letting her cook?"

I stuck my tongue out at them. "Shut up or I'll beam you with this breast." I waved the chicken threateningly, breading sprinkling on the floor, much to Odafin's delight.

Amera grabbed my wrist, supposedly to save the chicken. "That'd be the first set of titties Bastian's had in his face in a while," she cooed.

"Oh, you shut up, slut," Bastian retorted.

We all devolved into good-natured laughter. Amera flipped her braids, exposing a sleek, dark shoulder in her form-fitting tank. I watched Justin's eyes follow the movement, smile widening.

I managed to help Amera with dinner without destroying anything. Bastian had bought six bottles of wine, so the alcohol flowed freely and smoothed out everyone's hard edges. Bastian and Justin connected like they'd known each other for decades, which I took as a positive sign.

I was having such a good time that I almost forgot Justin's sultry look at Amera.

Once the food was done, we gathered around the kitchen table to eat like real, civilized adults. Justin picked at his plate while he quizzed Amera and Bastian on their majors and extracurricular activities. Amera's were Accounting, the honors program for Accounting majors, and finance director for her sorority. Bastian's were Digital Marketing and frat parties.

Since Justin was just picking at his plate, I was just picking, which earned me a series of hard stares from Amera for the duration of the meal. I just downed my wine.

The sweet wine wouldn't sit well on an empty stomach, but oh well.

After dinner, Amera cornered me at the sink where I was refilling my glass; the boys had moved back into the living room with a pack of cards.

"What the hell was that?"

I knew she was referring to my newfound peckishness. I might *be* fat, but I couldn't *act* fat in front of Justin, which meant going hungry. How could I possibly explain that to her?

"Let's just enjoy the wine!" I said instead, with a cheeriness I didn't feel.

She made a displeased *harrumping* sound, but dropped it because Bastian was waving us frantically over to the coffee table. He'd already set up the beer can and spread the cards out over the table facedown for a game of Kings.

Kings was one of my favorite drinking games because the rules were easy to remember and the opportunities for drinking were plentiful.

I grabbed the neck of the Moscato bottle and joined the boys on the floor, Amera following semireluctantly.

I was expecting many things to happen during our drinking game. I was expecting Amera to let slip some inside info about or concerning Justin that she wouldn't have been able to know without me telling her. I was expecting to have to do damage control.

I was not expecting the super obvious flirting Justin was laying on Amera, just right in front of me. I could tell no one else had expected it either. Bastian was looking sort of panicked and flustered. Amera was physically uncomfortable. She kept fidgeting with the neck of her tank and readjusting her hair and trying unsuccessfully to hide her hands. Since Justin had told her white was his favorite color in reference to her gel mani.

This bastard had his hand on my knee while he drooled over Amera.

Justin picked a card from the table and held it up. "Eight...is for date." He smiled. "I pick...Amera."

He took a small sip of his beer, Amera following with a sip of her wine. Her eyelids fluttered with a barely contained eye roll.

And why shouldn't he pick her over me? Who would pick me, seeing us both side by side? Not only was she stunning, she was smart, driven, accomplished, and excelled at everything I had ever seen her put her mind to. She was a fierce Aries, all the way down to her core.

The small throb of jealousy in my chest was a familiar feeling.

The game continued on like that, me trying to act like I was having a great time, until Bastian slid a card under the tab that popped the beer with a hiss.

"Finally," Bastian said with relief. Then he looked over at me and mouthed "sorry" which caused a flush of embarrassment to creep up my neck that I hoped everyone would just attribute to the wine.

Bastian didn't know quite as much about Justin's and my history, but he knew enough. Enough to feel sorry for me. It was unbearable.

"Well, night, everyone," I said.

I grabbed Justin's hand and was expecting to be met with resistance, but he just winked at Amera and followed me from the room.

Justin had never been to my space before. I definitely didn't let him come over to my mom's house, not that he'd ever asked. I usually just went to him.

I tried to see the room from his perspective and what it said about me. The overstuffed closet, whose door didn't shut all the way. The lava lamp Amera and I had found thrifting. The gauzy curtains. The dresser top, covered in jewelry, crystals, half-burnt candles, lotion, and perfume. Honestly, there were half-burnt candles on pretty much every free surface. The bed—which was made, mind you—covered in decorative pillows.

His hand brushed along my back.

"Gimme a minute."

Then he disappeared to the bathroom.

My heart hammered wildly in my chest, a mixture of nerves and giddy excitement. The last time we hooked up hadn't really been the best experience. I'd had too much to drink at a house party and in the early hours of the morning, I thought it was just me and him. But then one of his friends had walked in and I was too far gone to stop what had been brewing all night.

My accidental threesome was a great story for parties.

But I had put that night far, far behind me. Tonight, it was just us again.

Hastily, I ditched my dress and all constraining undergarments and pulled a cute set of lingerie from my dresser. Frilly and floral, they said cute and coquettish, cute but not bombshell, I'm not expecting anything but something would be nice. I added a little extra spritz of his favorite perfume to my neck.

I tossed the majority of the decorative pillows to the floor and climbed into the bed, rumpling the comforter up around me, so that I wasn't wholly exposed.

I pretended to scroll through my phone in an effort to still the frantic beating of my heart.

I shouldn't have bothered.

He took literally forever.

I was scrolling through my phone for real when he finally came back into the bedroom, shucked off his shoes, and flopped face-first down beside me, still fully clothed.

"Hey." He wriggled a little closer, nose going to my throat. "You smell nice."

"Mm-hmm." Scroll, scroll, scroll. The heat from his body was almost searing. I glanced down to see if I could gauge his mood in the light of my phone screen. His eyes were heavy-lidded and his forehead was pressed to my shoulder.

I tossed my phone down on the comforter. "I'm glad you came up today."

His lashes fluttered. "Yeah, me too. I liked meeting your friends. You always have the best friends."

I was reminded painfully of the way he seemed to shamelessly flirt with Amera. Like I wasn't sitting right there and watching everything.

"I got really lucky with Amera freshman year," I said, testing the waters.

He just mumbled something noncommittal and rolled onto his back, eyes closed.

"Are you okay?" He honestly hadn't had that much to drink, maybe a beer or two.

A soft smile curved his lips. "Yeah."

"Are you high?"

That got his attention and he propped up on an elbow. "Girl, no. I told you I don't do that anymore." He nuzzled my shoulder, the stubble on his face sending chills up and down my entire body.

But the feeling lingered in my stomach. He seemed so hot and cold today, and now he was languid and sleepy, when not an hour ago he had been boisterous and animated. I could never fucking tell. Every time I thought he was high, he would deny it, even if I would bet my soul I was right.

The nuzzling had stopped and Justin had fallen still again. Maybe he'd even passed out or fallen asleep.

The electricity buzzing through my body abruptly stopped, as if someone had suddenly flipped a switch.

I was not afraid of sex. I'd been having sex since I was fifteen and had many the partner since Justin. Some for just one night, some for a few months, some of it was bad, some of it was earth-shattering. The point being that I wasn't afraid to initiate sex or ask for whatever it was I wanted...usually. It was different with him. Justin always took the lead, always initiated first. I always waited patiently on tenterhooks, waiting for the sign, waiting for any sign that he wanted me as much as I wanted him. Sometimes it came and sometimes it didn't. Kind of like me.

The fact that he had failed to remove one stitch of clothing wasn't a good sign. Not the kind I looked for.

I wriggled down deeper into the pillows, so that we were more nose-to-nose. His breathing was even and close.

You know, fuck this noise.

I placed a kiss on his cheek and felt him smile. Emboldened, I moved down to his neck, bringing out my teeth for a little extra flair.

His hand landed softly on my waist. "I'm kinda tired right now, babe."

You have got to be fucking kidding me.

I immediately pulled back, chastised for the second time today.

He followed, wrapping his arms around my waist and pushing his head into my neck. Getting cozy, I guess. My body was stiff and unyielding. I felt like I couldn't breathe, couldn't move.

He placed another fucking chaste kiss on my dry lips. "You know you mean more to me than just sex, Vivi."

The use of that nickname tugged on something deep inside of me. Only two people ever used it: my dad and Justin.

He chuckled. "What were they calling you? Bryn? What's that about? You got a new identity?"

Yes and no. But it was too complicated to explain to him in the dark, especially since I didn't know if he was actually listening or not.

"Just a name I use at school."

"Oh, well, it's not as pretty as Vivien."

No, nothing and no one was as pretty as Vivien, on that we could agree.

CHAPTER FOUR

THE WRONG SWIPE

Dear Bryn,

I was hoping you would have some advice for someone sick and tired of playing the game. Long story short, I keep going to fraternity parties, making a great connection with a guy, exchanging numbers, going back to his place or mine, having a great time, and then poof. Nothing. Ghosted. It's happened three times! The common denominator seems to be me. But is it me??

Please help!

Sick and Tired

Ah, my sweet summer child. You have got to stop going to frat parties looking for a boyfriend. None of the guys you're meeting at the frat parties are looking for serious relationships. Do people meet at parties and eventually start a relationship? Sure. It happens. But repeat after me: we are the rule, not the exception.

You can't keep meeting these guys hoping one of them is going to be the exception, because the odds are slim.

Now, we at The Wrong Swipe are sex positive! If you want to check off all the frats on your Tap Card, please proceed with enthusiasm and make sure to keep it SSC (safe, sexy, and consensual).

But that doesn't sound like what you're wanting to do. So keep partying, but stop giving these guys any more of your time. You can always just stay for a quick and dirty make-out sesh—this columnist recommends the president's room at Eta Rho—but go home alone.

So let's talk about how and where to meet men of potential boyfriend material. First off, go to places and activities where all parties are sober. It sucks, I know, but you greatly increase your odds of finding someone on the same page as you, relationship-wise. Not to mention someone thinking with all available brain cells. Sorry, dudes.

Are you sporty and looking for someone sporty? Join an intramural league! Are you more studious? Check out the library! While I don't know his current status, there's a super cute curly-haired brunette working the reference desk on Fridays (hi, Eason). Are you a big nerd? The English Club hosts movie and video game nights all the time!

There are so many more options for you, Sick and Tired, and I can almost guarantee you will have better luck and be happier trying them out instead.

Also, if you find yourself in any of the above scenarios and are not sure what to do next, I have you covered! Check out my guide, 10 Ways to Start a Conversation, on our website: *pwuledger/thewrongswipe.com.*

CHAPTER FIVE

VIKINGBARD

Justin woke up obscenely early for someone who was "too tired" to do anything else, used the bathroom, and left.

I crawled back into bed, pulled the covers up over my head, and tried not to cry myself back to sleep.

I failed at that endeavor, so then just tried to make it quiet so that Amera wouldn't hear. I didn't know if I could survive her knowing look and raised eyebrows. I didn't think she would actually say "I told you so," but her expression would say "I told you so" nevertheless.

My nerves felt rubbed raw and exposed in a way I usually mutinously avoided. I had let him use me again, but for what, I had no idea. It certainly wasn't for sex.

I could usually identify exactly what I had been used for. Sex, money, a ride. But he had his own ride and hadn't asked for any money. Had he really come all this way just to hang out for a night and hit on my roommate?

The possibilities swirled around and around in my head like smoke; Justin was impossible to figure out so I reached out to someone who might be able to help.

Sheenah was my best friend from high school. We'd known each other since we were kids, and she'd been around to watch the whole Justin drama play out firsthand. The distance was hard, since she stayed in our hometown, but I still kept her in the loop about everything and always saw her when I went home.

I sent her a quick text. There's no way she'd be awake this early, but I could wait and wallow. I stuck my phone under my pillow and heard Odafin meow at the doorway.

I *psps psps*'ed him, patting a spot next to me on the bed. He was the only man I could really trust these days. Plus, he tolerated me aggressively cuddling him, which I did, tucking his warm, vibrating body up under my chin.

I hadn't even realized I'd fallen back asleep, hard, until Amera banged on the door. "It's afternoon, sleepyhead!"

I glanced at the time on my phone: 2:35. I was supposed to be at work at 3:00. *Oops.*

Ethan Rofkar was my twenty-five-year-old boss, The Bookery was his labor of love, and I ended up being only ten minutes late. We lived close.

When I came in, we did our usual song and dance.

Ethan said, "You're late."

I said, "Won't happen again!"

But we both knew that was a lie. Punctuality was not one of my strengths.

Ethan, with his swoopy Edward Cullen hair, couldn't afford more than a handful of employees. During our slow summer months, when everyone went home and the town hibernated, I was his only employee. So he begrudgingly tolerated me and my tardiness and snarky comments about his hair.

"You're looking especially magnificent today," I said, breezing past him at the coffee bar while trying to get my apron on. Let me tell you something: aprons are not a fat girl's best friend.

Ethan ran a hand over his swoop—over, not through, since there was too much gel involved for that.

"I need you to do the restocking today. Think you can manage?"

I saluted him. "Aye, *mi amor*."

"You can't call me that."

"Of course not, *sir*."

"Don't say it like that!"

I waved him off, the pink blush creeping from his ears down into his cheeks.

We kept the restock cart in the back—a collection of books and media people pulled out and couldn't be bothered to purchase or put away. Restocking was one of my favorite duties because I could thumb through all the books and pretend to be working. Ethan didn't mind when we were slow.

I wheeled the cart out, front wheel spinning and squeaking, just as the bell over the front door tinkled.

A customer would keep Ethan happy for the rest of the afternoon.

I pulled the first book off my cart and headed to the correct section. I was happily shelving books and humming along with the store radio when a male voice interrupted.

"I like your hair."

I whirled on him. "Excuse me?"

He stepped back. "I said, 'I like your hair.'"

"Oh, well, thanks."

Being the broke college student that I was, I couldn't afford frequent trips to the salon, which is why I had about five inches of root showing. The rest was electric green and teal, barely contained in a messy bun.

Then I realized I was staring at his nipples because I only came up to midchest. I had to tip my head back to see his grinning face. The man was a fucking tree.

He had a magnificent mane of tawny hair, a neatly cropped beard, and an armful of poetry books. Don't think I didn't also notice the way his biceps strained against the short sleeves of his gray V-neck. Panties, meet floor.

"I love you..." I trailed off, terribly distracted by his height and aggressive attractiveness. What I had *meant* to do was quote a line from one of my favorite Neruda sonnets. So much for that.

His thick lips split even wider, turning his grin almost goofy. "I'm flattered, but we've only just met." One of his large hands splayed dramatically on his chest. Oh yes, don't think I didn't notice how large his hands were.

"I didn't mean...obviously...Neruda." Very clever.

I gestured to one of the books he held.

"Oh, yes, Pablo. Just trying to get a jump start on my summer reading."

"You go to Penn Warren?" I crossed my arms under my expansive set of tits and watched his eyes as he noticed.

"Yeah," he said.

"Lemme guess. English Lit major?"

"With an emphasis in poetry, yeah." He cocked his head. "Do I know you?"

Oh, shit. My first thought was that I'd boned him and didn't remember. But no. He wasn't the kind of guy you'd just forget.

Please don't let him be a guy I've forgotten.

"I don't—"

"Yes! You write that advice column in the paper. I recognize you from your picture. Bryn, right?"

"Right, and you would be?"

"Toby Doan." I must have made a face because he added, "Tobias, if you want."

Oh, yes, me wants.

Tobias bought his books and left, taking my eyes with him.

I watched him from behind a set of shelves like a creep. He chatted jovially with Ethan, like they had known each other forever, which was impossible because I would have known if Ethan knew such a beautiful specimen.

Tobias Doan had the roundest ass I'd ever seen on a man.

His dark wash jeans clung snugly to his perfectly round ass and perfectly sculpted thighs. He stood with his legs braced apart, I'm assuming to account for those thighs and who knew what else. It should be illegal to look that good in a pair of jeans.

I resisted the urge to fan myself with my hand or one of the nearby books. I refused to swoon like some Southern Belle.

My phone buzzed just as Tobias exited the bookstore. Finally, a distraction.

It was Sheenah, finally responding to my obscenely early morning text.

VIVIEN

CALL ME ON BREAK xoxo

I poked my head out from behind the shelf. "Ethan, I'm taking my fifteen!"

He gave me an extremely dorky thumbs-up.

I hit dial on Sheenah's contact on the way to the back break room slash storage room.

She picked up on the first ring. "Vivien, oh my God. What did the douche nozzle do this time?"

I sighed at the familiar comfort of her sparkly voice. "It's good to hear your voice, Shee."

I was overcome with a wash of emotion I had finally been able to identify as homesickness. Justin seemed to do that to me. Always brought me back to that fifteen-year-old girl in her small hometown with dreams of getting out. Always made me miss the familiar and comfortable people I had spent the majority of my life with.

Amera and Sebastian and my other college friends were dear to me, but they were new and shiny.

Talking to Sheenah felt like putting on an oversized, well-worn sweater—safe and warm.

"How are you?" I asked.

I could feel her impatience through the phone. "I only have a few minutes before my shift. You gotta talk fast. We can catch up on normal things later."

So I tried to tell her everything that had happened in the last day.

"Ugh," she said.

Honestly, same.

"When are you going to stop picking up the phone, baby doll? This always happens. He always lets you down."

Great, now she was sounding just like Amera.

But she wasn't finished.

"You've got to stop accepting these fucking crumbs and calling it a loaf. You're worth more than he's willing to give, obviously."

How *dare*. How dare she use my own words against me. I had written a long tirade about crumbing last week.

I could feel the tightness in my face of tears brewing again. But I wasn't going to be one of those bitches who cried at work. I curled one of my hands into a tight fist of frustration, pointy nails digging into my palm.

"Sheenah, you don't—"

"Fuck him, Vivien. You are better than this."

And that would be the ironic part. Because I wasn't so sure I was. I wasn't so sure I was worth more than Justin was willing to give.

After my shift ended, I picked up a sandwich from the deli next door to The Bookery and caught the university's bus system back to the house.

I beat Amera home, which was unusual, since she normally didn't work as late as me. She'd managed to snag a snazzy internship with a local CPA firm, which was going to give her a huge boost after graduation.

Thinking about after graduation plans sent a thread of guilt running through me. My personal essay was still calling my name. I was applying to a prestigious and highly competitive journalism internship in Boston that would start next May, if I were lucky.

My advisor had been helping me through the application and she said my odds were good, but I had to nail the statement. Nail it like no personal statement had ever been nailed before.

I sighed again, eyeing the state of our living room and kitchen. We hadn't cleaned up after our impromptu house party last night and you could tell.

Grabbing a black garbage bag, I went around picking up empty bottles, various food detritus, and paper plates and napkins. I attacked the dirty wineglasses next, made a sink of hot soapy water, and wiped down the counters, table, and coffee table. I emptied the dishwasher before sitting down at the kitchen table to eat my sandwich.

Amera would be so proud of me.

Not five minutes later, Amera stomped through the door and thumped her bag down so hard on the table that my water glass shivered.

"Bad day?" I raised my eyebrows.

She slumped into the chair across from me.

"I think I got smelled by my boss," she said, in a tone that was better suited for telling me what she had for lunch.

I paused, mouth open and poised for a bite. "He did what now?"

"He stood way too close behind me after our morning meeting and swear to God he smelled my hair."

From what I could tell, the only interns at Amera's firm were her and a pompous white boy. I doubt the pompous white boy was getting smelled by Creepy Boss.

Creepy Boss had been a mild annoyance since Amera started, standing too close, lingering too long, watching too hard. He gave her all the best assignments and let her sit in on high-level meetings with clients, the cost being tolerating his questionable behavior.

"Do you want me to investigate him? I could write a scathing, anonymous take down in the *Ledger*. I would eviscerate him for you."

She smiled and her eyes gleamed. "Nah, I have a plan."

"Well, if you need an alibi, let me know."

"I'm just going to work circles around his lily ass, get my recommendation letter, and surpass him in the field. Maybe I'll even take his job one day."

"Will you tell HR if it gets worse?" While I fully supported Amera's revenge plot, I didn't want anything to happen to her at work. Or for her older, white male boss to tank her prospects in retaliation.

She nodded her head, reaching across the table and snagging the butcher paper my sandwich was wrapped in, pulling it towards her.

I swatted at her. "Hey!"

"You owe me." She gave me a pointed look and I knew she meant I owed her for the Justin debacle. I sighed and relinquished the other half of my sandwich as penance.

"Do you want to talk about it?" she asked, picking off green peppers.

I took a less-than-bracing gulp of water. There wasn't anything I could say to explain what had happened.

Amera took a bite of my sandwich. "You know it took literally every ounce of self-control I possess not to say anything to him, right? I did that for you, not him."

I stared at the tabletop and said quietly, "I know."

Tucked up in bed, I was performing my nightly social media scroll. Facebook was family-only, so I spent most of my time on Instagram. I had posted a few casual selfies since my birthday, but the birthday selfie and pictures of me, Amera, and Bastian were still getting the most likes.

Today's selfie was me with my huge sunglasses on out in front of The Bookery with the caption, *Welcome to summer!* Emoji, emoji, emoji.

Two new notifications popped up as I was scrolling. Ooh, I had a new follower.

Vikingbard is now following you.

Vikingbard would like to send you a message.

Without even clicking on the profile, I had a sneaking suspicion that I already knew exactly who vikingbard was.

Before accepting his message, I went to his profile to take a look around. His feed was mostly books, landscapes, houseplants, quoted poetry, and the occasional artistic selfie here and there, showcasing his hard jawline.

More notifications were pouring in. Vikingbard was going through my feed and liking the last few days of posts.

I was intrigued, so I finally followed him back and accepted his messaging request.

I'd like to continue the conversation we started earlier. The one where you said you loved me

Against my better judgement, a smile tugged at my lips.

I only love Neruda. Sorry

He was apparently online because his response came fast.

I'm impressed with your knowledge of Neruda

Yes, I live to impress random dudes in bookstores

Sassy, I like it

My fingers hovered over the keypad on my phone. There was no doubt Tobias Doan was flirting with me.

The issue was whether I was going to take his bait and flirt back. I must have been taking too long to decide because another message came in from him.

Can I have your number? I want to ask you on a date but doing it over dm feels…cliché

And I am far from cliché

Oh really? You seem pretty cliché for a poet

How many poets do you know?

Irl? None, honestly

As I suspected. Number?

Now I was openly grinning at my phone like a stupid fool. Not a minute after I provided my phone number, a text message came in.

Now, that's better

I decided to have a little fun.

Who's this?

He sent a string of frowny faces and one crying emoji.

Just kidding. Sorry lol

Oh, you think you're funny

Yeah, sometimes

I think you're funny. I enjoy reading your column

I suddenly felt a surge of self-consciousness. I was fiercely protective of my column and my readers and men tended not to be my biggest fans, mostly because I spent a lot of time calling them on their bullshit. I received my fair share of messages and DMs calling me a bitch, a harpy, a fat bitch, and a dozen other horribly uninspired names. Block.

Uh, thanks

So...about that date

You are very direct

No time like the present, eh

Oh, and you had me at hello

How's that

That is a big fat CLICHÉ

Yeah, sorry

You still haven't answered my question

Are you stalling?

I promise I'm not creepy

The funny thing was that I was actually stalling.

Tobias was hot, there was no denying that. And he was apparently interested and funny and charming and persistent. I conjured up the feelings from last night and this morning. The way I had to curl into myself, again, and cry myself to sleep, again. How

I felt so much less than. How Justin hadn't even texted me today at all.

Ok, yes, I will go out with you
This pleases me :)

CHAPTER SIX

TWIX AND MILK DUD

Tobias and I set up our date for the upcoming Saturday at two o'clock in the afternoon. What the hell were we going to do at two o'clock in the afternoon?

I assumed he was going to take me to dinner. That seemed to be the traditional first date option. Maybe we'd have dinner after whatever super-secret activity we were doing in the afternoon?

I harangued the man for details, but he wouldn't budge.

How am I supposed to know what to wear if you won't tell me what we are doing? This is v important!

My lips are sealed

Just be comfortable

Great. Just great. My level of comfort varied greatly depending on the activity. I was willing to sacrifice comfort for style on many occasions as well, if the situation called for it.

Saturday dawned bright and hot—it was so fucking hot outside.

I had managed to get absolutely zero additional details from Tobias, which, honestly, was really working in his favor, since I was intensely curious and intrigued, even if slightly frustrated.

Amera was sitting on my bed, watching me struggle with options. Arguing with myself.

"It's in the middle of the afternoon, so obviously nothing fancy, right?"

She shrugged. "Probably not. Why are you worrying so much about it?"

"It's the first date."

"Right. Just the one. And he's already seen you. He knows what you look like." Her words weren't harsh, just matter of fact.

I nibbled my bottom lip. As always, Amera knew how to get right to the crux of the issue without even really trying.

Tobias knows what I look like.

And he asked me out anyway.

And he saw me when I wasn't looking all that put together anyway.

And he saw all of me.

Not just a perfectly cropped and curated profile picture.

He knew what he was getting into.

In the end, I picked a strappy midlength sundress and a brown pair of faux-Birkenstocks. I went light on the makeup since it was the middle of the day and fucking hot, and put my hair up in a loose pony.

Tobias didn't have a car—we had that in common already—so we had agreed to meet at the university bus stop that was only one street over from my house. It was my usual stop.

I got to the stop only a few moments before Tobias; I had the chance to watch him walk up from the direction of campus before he spotted me.

When he did, his face broke out into a luminous smile that made my belly flop. He was wearing basically the same outfit as our first meeting, except this time the V-neck T-shirt was cerulean blue and better emphasized his tan.

He pulled ear buds from his ears when he got to me and stuffed them in his pocket. "Hey."

"Do you own any other shirts?"

Well, that was bitchy, but it slipped from my mouth anyway.

He just laughed, deep and genuine. "Honestly? Not really." He ran a hand down his flat stomach. "When I find something I like, I tend to stick to it."

"What were you listening to?"

"A local indie band. You probably don't know them. Not many people do."

I nodded. "Yeah, I'm more of a Taylor Swift girl myself." I rocked a bit on my feet as we waited for the bus. "So, are you going to tell me where we're going yet?"

He stepped a little closer to me, and I couldn't tell if it was deliberate or if he was just adjusting his stance. He smelled fresh and zesty. His own wavy hair was up in a messy man bun on top of his head.

"Nope. It's a surprise."

The bus approached with a rumble and we both showed our student IDs as we got on and Tobias chose a seat in the middle. I followed him, but decided to sit in the seat directly in front. I wasn't quite ready for him to find out how much space I took up on a bus seat.

He propped his large arms on the top of my seat and leaned forward.

"So, you never told me your major. You know mine."

I propped a leg up on the seat so I could face him. "Journalism with a minor in Advertising and Broadcasting."

"Ah." His slate blue eyes sparkled and I had to concentrate hard to not just stare at him in fascination. "I should have known. Do you do anything with the radio station?"

"Yeah, I've been on before as a commentator, but that's all. It's notoriously hard to break in and do anything else. All the spots are usually taken by Broadcasting majors and stay that way."

"Are you a senior?"

"Yep. Officially for the fall."

He grinned. "Oh, hey, me too."

I wanted to ask him what exactly he was planning to do with a poetry degree, but I felt like that was probably a rude question, so I'd save it for later. Honestly, he could probably say the same thing about my journalism degree, so that can of worms was better left unopened.

The bus rolled to a stop. "Here's our stop!"

Tobias let me get off the bus first and hopped off the last step.

We were in the middle of an old town square that was mostly boutique shops for tourists mixed in with some small local restaurants. It wasn't a section of town I was really familiar with. I didn't have much need to come here.

"So, where to now?"

"It's just a bit farther."

With that he took my hand and started walking down a shady sidewalk. Well, at least there was some damn shade. His hand was hot and nearly totally engulfed mine.

True to his word, we didn't have to go far. Just down the street until the buildings opened up.

Tobias pulled me off the sidewalk and onto a gravel driveway. Shit, was this the part where I got murdered?

But it wasn't much farther and then I saw the sign: Sumpter County Animal Shelter.

I tried to withhold judgement until we got inside. A twiggy girl with pink buzzed hair greeted us at the reception area.

"Toby!" Her smile was wide and familiar.

"Hey, Tamra, you got them?"

"Sure do!"

With that she went into the back, where I'm assuming the kennels were kept, and returned with a pair of fat, roly-poly, floppy-eared, fuzzy, German shepherd puppies.

She handed one to Tobias and one to me. I cradled the puppy to my chest and it licked my face.

Tamra was still talking. "They're really too small for leashes, so just take them out back and let them run around for a bit."

"Great." He flashed a smile and then led me out a side door to a grassy, fenced area.

I held my puppy on my chest like it was the most precious thing in the world, which, duh, it was, and inhaled that sweet, sweet puppy smell.

Tobias set his puppy down and it immediately took off, but tripped over its too-big feet. He glanced at me. "You can let her down."

I scratched her ears. "No, I can't."

He laughed again and I couldn't help the huge grin that spread over my face. I could almost cry because the puppies were just that cute.

I kissed mine's forehead before setting her down, where she promptly went and rolled over her friend.

"How did you know they were here?"

"I walk the dogs at least once a week. Tamra told me they'd been surrendered last week. I'm honestly surprised they haven't been adopted yet. I thought you would like them."

He glanced over at me, I'm assuming to gauge my reaction. I don't know what he saw—probably me crying with joy.

"I love them," I whispered.

We sat down in the grass together and the puppies came and chewed on our shoes. I didn't even care. One of them lay down between my legs and I rubbed her belly.

My phone buzzed and I pulled it out, only because I was expecting a text from Amera.

She was right on time.

Are you still alive? Yay or nay?

Yay. Winky face emoji

She sent back a string of heart eyes.

I exited messaging and opened my camera app instead. "Hey, is it okay if I take a few pictures? I totally won't if it's not cool with Tamra or the shelter."

"The shelter could use some publicity. Are you one of those influencer people?"

"Eh, not really." I had a fairly large following, but nothing that would make me an influencer. But most of my followers were locals and college girls who I'm sure loved puppies. "Do they have names?"

"This one is Twix," he said, picking up one of the puppies. "And this one with the spot is Milk Dud."

Milk Dud was the puppy I had first. I must admit, she did resemble a little glob of chocolate. "Who named them?"

"Me. Tamra lets me name all the new arrivals."

Interesting. I'd have to get the scoop on his relationship with Tamra later; right now I had puppies to wrangle for their photo shoot.

Tobias was, surprisingly, a very helpful assistant photographer. Most dudes go screaming in the other direction when you pull the camera out. Or roll their eyes and huff. Tobias did neither. He helped me arrange the puppies, take picture after picture of me with them, and even posed for a few pictures himself.

Tobias cradling a fat puppy in his big, gentle hands was like, damn. My ovaries about burst. If this didn't get them adopted, nothing would.

We returned Twix and Milk Dud to Tamra and I told her about my plan.

"Yes, girl. Tag the shelter! We could always use more donations and volunteers."

On our way back up the street, I said, "I hope they get adopted."

Tobias hadn't grabbed my hand again and that was disappointing. "I'm sure they will. I'll let you know when they do."

"I hope so soon." It broke my heart to leave Milk Dud in the shelter, and everything in my willpower not to take her home myself. But we didn't have space for a dog, and the last thing I needed was another life form to keep alive.

I had enough trouble with myself. Which reminded me of all the houseplant pictures Tobias had on his Instagram.

"Hey, do you like...plants?" Well, that was smooth and not awkward at all.

He grinned down at me. "Yep. I collect them."

"Oh, cool."

I mentally tallied up what I knew about Tobias so far: was a poet, loved dogs, a college boy that volunteered at a shelter in his free time, collected houseplants and apparently had the wherewithal to keep them alive.

"Do you want to get ice cream? There's a cute little shop in the square."

Did I want to get ice cream? Of course I wanted to get ice cream. Had he seen the swing of these hips?

With any other guy I would issue an emphatic no, I do not want any ice cream, why no, I am not hungry at all, I do not require sustenance to sustain life. I exist on air, protein bars, and fatphobia.

But things felt different with Tobias. I felt like I could be honest and that was a dangerous game. I'd have to bring the walls back up, but for now, I said, "Yes, I would love ice cream."

True to his word, there was a little shop right across from the square called Annie's Big Scoop. It was filled with ice cream ephemera, blessedly cold air-conditioning, and everything was either pink or white. Cute, indeed.

The shop was bursting with small, frilly white tables and very delicate-looking, filigreed chairs. Before I could even spend much time contemplating whether to chance sitting down on one of the tiny chairs, Tobias suggested we eat our ice cream out by the fountain.

The fountain was in the middle of the square and nicely shaded, so it wasn't a bad idea at all.

We grabbed our ice cream and sat on the large concrete lip of the decorative fountain.

Our knees tilted perilously close to each other; there was barely an inch separating them. We ate our ice cream in comfortable silence.

First, puppies. Now, ice cream.

There was definitely something wrong with him. There had to be. Or else I had accidentally stumbled upon the elusive unicorn of men. And I just didn't think my luck was that good.

Maybe he was just biding his time before sticking me in a hole and starving me so he could wear my skin as a people suit.

I wiped my fingers delicately with the little white napkins we'd taken from the shop.

"That was delicious, thank you," I said.

He was staring at me intensely. *Yup, definitely getting stuck in a hole.*

"You have something..." His hand lifted and he wiped whatever it was off my chin. Then he brought his thumb to his mouth and licked it clean.

At the swipe of his tongue, heat flooded my entire body like the fucking Nile.

"Yum, minty." He smiled again, but it was different this time. Slyer, hotter, like he knew exactly what he'd just done. Like he knew exactly what I was now thinking about doing to that thumb.

"Mint's my favorite," I breathed.

"Can I kiss you?"

God, he better fucking kiss me after that show. Instead, I just nodded because I didn't trust myself to speak anything of any coherence or intelligence. It'd been a while since I'd had a first kiss that was sober, and it would be my first kiss out in the middle of broad daylight, so I wasn't sure what to expect.

I was not expecting *that*.

His lips were on mine almost immediately, his hand sliding behind my head. My first thought was *ew, sweaty*, but then he clamped down, gently, on my neck and my breath hitched.

His lips were deliciously warm and soft and they moved with precision and care. He led, and I followed.

I was suddenly very aware that his free hand had landed on my thigh, his hot palm searing near through the wispy fabric of my dress. I returned the gesture, bracing both of my hands on both of his thighs. As I suspected, they were solid as steel. His muscles jumped at my touch.

His fingers flexed on my neck.

I grabbed his thick bottom lip with my teeth and a moan rumbled deep in his throat.

There was a shuffling noise that distracted us, and I abruptly pulled back.

Two older ladies in pastel-colored capris and big hats had stopped in their journey from boutique to boutique and were trying—and failing—not to stare.

I supposed I'd stare too if I saw two people getting hot and heavy on the side of a public fountain.

I gave them a small wave and they scurried away.

Tobias just laughed and the husky sound warmed me from head to toe. I had a great desire to pick up where we left off. We hadn't even started with any tongue yet.

"I guess I should get you home safely," Tobias said, standing.

Oh. It had only been a few hours.

So soon? Maybe he hadn't been as affected by our kiss as I was? I was many things; one of which was not a bad kisser. All of my reviews on that front had been stellar.

I stood and shook out my dress. "Oh, yeah, okay, sure."

I tried not to give away any of the swirling emotions inside me at the moment.

He grabbed my hand again as we walked back to the bus stop.

True to his word, Tobias saw me right up to my front steps. I attempted to make a quick escape, but he tugged on my hand.

"Hey, you didn't say goodbye."

Slightly off-balance, I bumped into his rock wall of a chest. His very solid arms encased my waist, leaving me not much choice other than to do the same.

I looked up. Way up. "Well, goodbye, Tobias Doan."

His eyes sparkled with mirth. "Bryn St. Jean, you wound me." His head tilted towards mine and his warm breath drifted across my face. I resisted the urge to sigh. He was so warm, but not uncomfortably so. Just warm enough to set my skin tingling. "That's it, after everything? I used up all my best moves."

"Oh, I thought..." I did a little shoulder shrug. "You ended our date. At the good part."

He laughed. "I'm sorry, I've got the evening shift at the front desk of King Hall." His arms squeezed. "Believe me, I would have...enthusiastically continued." His voice had gone so deep and dark and full of promises.

My heart stuttered and I resisted the urge to say something stupid or nonsensical, even though my head was literally just full of images of Tobias's lips and hands and an imagining of what he would look like naked.

I pushed up on my toes and planted a quick kiss on those lips instead. "Good."

I scurried away before he could do anything else and was left with an image of him, arms flung wide, a grin on his face, and him shouting, "That's it!" at my retreating back.

CHAPTER SEVEN

FUCKING PEPEROMIA

Bastian was plopped on the couch when I entered. He was shirtless and had his feet propped up on the coffee table, watching a reality TV show.

"How'd you get in here?"

He popped a chip. "Window."

Unbeknownst to everyone except Bastian, one of the living room windows had a defunct lock that fell open if you jiggled it in the right way.

"You're home early." He wiggled his eyebrows.

"Oh, shut it." I plopped down next to him and seized the bag of chips. "Those are our chips, freeloader!"

"Whatever, you love me."

"Only because you always bring the booze."

Bastian flung his arm around my head and looked at me expectantly. "So? You really think you can just come in here and not say anything?"

I didn't even have to ask how he knew about my date with Tobias. If you told one twin something, the other twin would always find out eventually.

"It's my house!"

"Pfft."

I leaned into his warm side. "Where is your shirt?"

"When you look as good as I do, shirts are optional."

I snorted. "I doubt Amera would agree with you. She'd probably have something to say about all that exposed flesh on our couch."

He turned his attention back to the housewives. "It's not the worst thing that's been on your couch."

"Oh, gross, Bastian!"

He just smirked and kept eating our chips.

I toed off my sandals and curled up tighter under his arm, taking my phone out of the pocket of my dress.

I had stayed off my phone for the majority of our date, which really said something about Tobias, so I had some catching up to do.

As I suspected, my puppy photo shoot was a big hit and I had several comments about going to rescue Twix and Milk Dud RIGHT NOW. That made me extremely happy.

To my surprise, I already had a text from Tobias. He hadn't even waited an hour.

Had a great time. Do it again soon? Smiley face emoji.

I debated making him wait a little bit for a response. But Tobias hadn't struck me as the kind of guy to play games. He seemed refreshingly honest. He asked for what he wanted. And I'd be a liar if I tried to pretend I didn't want to see him again and kiss him again and see what else that kissing led to.

I'm not sure you can top that date, but I'd be willing to let you try
You underestimate my powers
I bet
If we bet on it, what do I win?
I smiled. He was tempting. So, so tempting.
For shame, Mr. Doan. I am a respectable girl
I'd respect the hell out of you...respectfully
Oh, we were entering dangerous territory. I'm not sure he knew quite what he was getting into. Phone sex was one of my favorite activities. I had a whole gallery of sexy pictures ready to deploy when the occasion called for it.

"Are you sexting?"

I clamped the phone to my chest. "Don't be reading my messages!"

Bastian grinned. "I didn't. Your face got red and you have this stupid smile on your face, so I only assumed that's what you're doing."

"I'm not sexting! We've only had one date." Not that that's stopped me before.

"That hasn't stopped you before."

I punched him good-naturedly in the shoulder. Bastian had the audacity to look affronted. "Hey, no judgement from me."

My phone buzzed with another text from Tobias.

I'm sorry. Was that too much?

Ah, shit. I had let the moment go and now it was weird.

No, sorry, roommates

Ah, roommates. I don't have any roommates. Just fyi

Duly noted. Winky face.

"I think I might like this one," I said.

"So you only sext the ones you don't like?"

"You know how boys are. You're either a whore or a Madonna and there's no middle ground."

Bastian sighed. "Yes, unfortunately I know how boys are."

"So tell me what I should do. If I fuck him too fast, I'm easy, and if I make him wait too long, I'm a prude."

"Girl, you're the relationship expert."

I snorted. "An advice column doesn't make an expert. Obviously."

"So, what would you tell you?"

"I'd tell me that if he was going to hit it and quit it, he was going to do it no matter what. First date or third date."

Bastian spread his hands out, like I had just revealed the secrets of the universe. "There's your answer. You do you, girl."

Yes, unfortunately I had written that advice on numerous occasions, but I still got letters about girls struggling about when to give up the goods. Why buy the cow when you got the milk for free and all that bullshit. Did boys ever have to struggle about when to give up the goods? Not in my experience. They did what they wanted, when they wanted. No one ever compared them to cows. They could give away all the free milk they wanted.

I texted Sheenah. *I had a first date and didn't sleep with him*

That, my friend, is what we call growth

Lol you wouldn't be saying that if you saw him

Was it that mammoth in your insta pic????

Shit girl nvm hit that shit

I held up the phone so Bastian could see the messages. "See, Sheenah thinks I should hit that."

"Are you just going to poll all your friends?"

"Maybe."

"Just follow your vagina...er, heart."

No, he was right. My heart had nothing to do with the feelings Tobias inspired, despite the way it pounded furiously when we kissed.

Our second date was less of a second date and more of an informal invitation to meet him at the front desk of King Hall the very next night.

It was already almost nine, so I dressed a little spicier for the occasion. I decided to pull out the big guns and dragged on my only pair of skinny jeans and a peplum leopard print top with the requisite deep scoop neck. The peplum would hide the way the waistband of my jeans dug into my middle.

I swiped my student ID to get into King Hall and it was completely empty, save for Tobias behind the front desk. His booted feet were propped on the desk and he was absorbed in a rather thick book. He didn't even look up when I entered. Some front desk guard he was.

I sauntered over. "Nothing getting past you, huh."

A smile immediately lit up his face. "Hey."

"What are you reading?"

He set the book down. "Literary theory—"

I gagged. "Uh, gross."

"No, it's actually really interesting—"

I held up a hand to stop him. "Please, spare me." I glanced around the empty lobby and common area pointedly. "What are you even doing here? I didn't think anyone stayed in the dorms during the summer."

"Just King Hall. High schoolers for the summer gifted programs."

"Oh, God. There are children here?"

He glanced at his phone. "Curfew's at nine. So they should be mostly in their rooms."

"They're my problem, now," an unfamiliar voice rumbled.

While we had been talking, a large Black guy wearing a goldenrod yellow, branded Penn Warren T-shirt had sidled up beside me.

"Hey, man," Tobias greeted. "This is Tanner, my night shift. Tanner, Bryn, Bryn, Tanner."

"Bryn from The Wrong Swipe?"

"That's me."

"Oh, man, I love your column!"

Well, I liked Tanner immediately.

"You got me my girlfriend."

My eyebrows rose. "Really? How'd I do that?"

"She wrote you a letter about having a crush on the guy sitting in front of her in her econ class. That was me. You told her it was patriarchal bullshit to sit around waiting for me to make the first move and recommended she find a way to start talking to me. The next day she asked me for a pen."

"Ah, yes, the old pen maneuver. Always happy to help a reader."

"You're doing the Lord's work, Bryn, keep it up."

I laughed. "I've never heard it put quite that way before."

"You got this, man?" Tobias handed Tanner a heavy set of keys to who knows what. To me, he said, "I need to run to my room real quick. Wanna come up?"

A series of quick smiles passed between the boys; Tanner at least had the decency to put his head down and try to hide his in his chest.

Tobias gathered his stuff and I followed him to the elevators.

"So how many girls has Tanner seen you bring up?"

He sputtered and that was exactly the reaction I was going for. I didn't honestly care how many girls Tobias had dated or slept with or done whatever with. I just wanted to see him squirm for a bit.

He hit the button for the fifth floor. I leaned against the back of the elevator and crossed my arms and raised my immaculate brows, awaiting his answer.

He looked at me sidelong, some, but not all, of the humor gone from his face. "What kind of answer do you want? A real one, or a diplomatic one?"

Hmm, this should be interesting. "A real one."

"Honestly, I just ended a six-year relationship with my high school girlfriend a few months ago. So, uh, none. Except you." His smile bounced back.

"Oh." Guess I was the only slut in this dynamic.

I did the math. If we were about the same age, he would have been with the same girl since fifteen or sixteen. Assuming their relationship was closed and exclusive, he'd only had sex with one girl. Meanwhile, I had to keep a list of names in my phone so I didn't accidentally forget anyone.

I tried to figure out if that changed the way I felt about Tobias.

The elevator chimed and I watched the way his ass moved under his fitted jeans.

Nope. It didn't change shit.

Tobias explained to me that he had been a Resident Advisor since the beginning of junior year. He got a single occupancy room for his efforts, but still had to use the community bathroom. Ew. Hence why I had moved out of the dorms with Amera as soon as humanly possible.

I made a great show of checking out his space.

He'd pushed the two single beds together to make one super bed, neatly made with plaid sheets and exactly two pillows. The plaid made sense. I could definitely see him wearing a helluva lot of plaid in the winter. His desk was neat, as was the countertop of his sink. His hair and beard products were lined up in neat little rows. I was impressed with the hair care products; this was a man who knew his way around hair. Which would definitely explain why his always looked so nice and silky and tuggable.

Tobias put his literary theory textbook back on a small bookshelf.

"Why did you want to be an RA?"

He shrugged. "I like people. And I got this sweet bachelor pad."

"Hmm."

In front of the window was a large shelf filled with plants. Again, very neatly organized in their multicolored terra-cotta pots. "The plants!"

I went to take a closer look and Tobias followed.

"So, these are the Sansevieria, these are golden pothos, this guy is a Fern Victoria, this little one is a Peperomia Golden Gate, and the ones at the top are succulents." He ran his fingers over the leaves of one of them. "This one is looking kind of peckish."

It took all my self-control not to giggle. I put my hand over my mouth. Here was this giant-ass man with his ripped arms, mother-henning over a collection of nonsentient foliage. It was freaking adorable—and refreshing. I wouldn't have to pretend to be interested in sports. I just had to find out what a fucking Peperomia was.

"Are you laughing at me?"

"No, I swear." I still had to hold my hand over my mouth to stifle my laughter. "It's very cute."

His answer was a grunt in the style of Geralt of Rivia.

"I mean, I have no idea what you said, but still cute, nonetheless." I gently patted the pot of the one I was pretty sure was a fern. "They are very nice."

"Just wait. I'll convert you into a plant person in no time."

"No way. You don't want to put anything living into my care. Not if you want it to stay alive." Odafin was the one exception. Only because he was particularly obnoxious about being fed regularly and on time.

"These are all easy-care. They're tough." He ran a long finger along the edge of one of the shelves.

I had a feeling he wasn't deliberately trying to be erotic. But the care and ease in which his finger moved sent a ripple down my spine. I couldn't take my eyes off him. He moved with surprising grace for a man of his size.

I also could think of a hundred better uses for his fingers.

I coughed. "Uh, so, what do you wanna do?"

He turned that burning gaze on me, and the dark smile was back. He took a step closer, the heat from his body engulfing mine.

"Whatever you want."

His voice was low and husky. I could feel my lips part of their own volition, my breath quickening. *Whatever I wanted.* I wanted to press my face to his chest and inhale until I was drowning in his smell and his skin. I wanted to kiss him again. A kiss to rival all kisses.

I knew, deep in my belly, that the ball was firmly in my court. I knew I could walk out of this room with no consequences. I knew I could have him take me to a fancy dinner, so that way at least, I wouldn't be giving up something for nothing. I knew I could have what I really wanted, here, now, in this moment.

I drew in a deep breath that moved my whole chest. He wasn't even touching me yet and my whole body was tingling. He just watched me with those deep, dark, swirling storm-blue eyes.

I clenched my hands. I noticed they were trembling. *Get your shit together.* I wasn't some blushing maiden. I was a whole-ass grown woman and what I wanted was to touch a whole-ass grown man.

I reached a hand out, running my nails down the length of his forearm. I stopped at his wrist, rubbing the soft underside with my thumb. His fingers twitched.

"Kiss me again."

He did not need to be told twice.

Tobias wrapped both arms around my waist, crushing me to his hard body. His lips went immediately to mine and boy, was he holding back the first time around. The second kiss pulled no punches. It was hard and fast, demanding and devouring. I slipped my arms around his neck, one hand tangling in his hair. He liked that. Both hands clamped down on my ass, pulling me even closer, if that was even possible.

His tongue slipped through my lips and I moaned.

Well, he sure accomplished that a whole hell of a lot faster than I was expecting.

I drew my hands down his neck, over his broad shoulders, down his arms. My fingers ached with the desire to touch him, to explore every nook and cranny.

I skimmed the space between his stomach and the waistband of his jeans, and he made a growling sound deep in his throat.

Pleased, my hands slipped under his shirt and landed on the ridged planes of his stomach. The muscles quivered at my touch.

We finally broke the kiss, but his eyes lingered on my lips and I almost couldn't breathe. I nearly lost my nerve. I grabbed the edge of his shirt and slowly pulled it up, ever so slowly so he could stop me anytime he wanted to.

He didn't.

He stared. And waited.

He was deliciously compliant as I tugged the shirt up and over his head, his mane swinging free from the collar.

Son of a bitch.

Tobias's skin was a soft bronze covered by soft light blond hair. I knew it was soft because I literally couldn't stop my hands from touching his abdomen again. I counted them with my hands. One, two, three, four, five, six, seven, eight. The man had an eight-pack. He was like nothing I'd ever seen before. Hard and soft simultaneously. My fingers slipped into the grooves over his hip bones.

And then I had to take a step back so I could catch my breath. "Jesus."

"What?" He looked very disappointed that I had stopped my exploring.

Fuck, did I say that out loud? Whoops.

"You have"—I made a V-shaped gesture with my hands—"an Adonis belt."

"A what?" He looked down.

"You have the V! The V lines!" I sounded almost hysterical. Where did this guy even come from? A *Men's Health* magazine?

With no help from my mother, I had spent years trying to undo the hate she had helped cultivate towards my body. This body could do amazing things. This body felt amazing things. It had yet to let me down, freshman fifteen or not.

The desire bubbling in my stomach abruptly fizzled out. The guys I slept with categorically *did not* look like Tobias. They were all smaller than me, yes, but they also all tended to have softer, rounded bellies. None of this eight-pack nonsense.

His thick brows furrowed. "Bryn, what's wrong?"

There was nothing wrong with him, obviously. It's not like I had never seen a guy with abs before. Guys with abs hit me up all the time. But I knew better than to take that bait. Guys that looked like Tobias did not see anything serious in girls that looked like me.

So then I had to decide if one night with Tobias was worth it.

He had picked his shirt back up from the floor and was about to put it back on.

"No, wait."

Stop being a pansy bitch, I chided myself. I had broken the mood and I needed to reverse course, quickly. Tobias probably already thought there was something wrong with me.

There probably *was* something wrong with me, but that was beside the point. The point was that I had an insanely hot, half-naked boy ready to jump my bones, and I had to freak out and almost ruin everything.

"Hold that thought. I just...have to pee."

I definitely did not have to pee, but I scurried to the communal bathroom anyway. Thankfully, Tobias's room was almost directly across from one.

The bathroom was just like I remembered them: two stalls, two showers, and two sinks nestled in one long vanity.

I leaned against the vanity with both hands and took a good long look at the girl in the smudged mirror.

It was pep talk time.

"You are a hot bitch. He would be lucky to have you."

I stared her down. The plump cheeks were flushed. Lips swollen from Tobias's amorous attentions, fucking expensive lipstick barely smudged. With a pinky finger, I quickly wiped away some of the excess.

Voices coming closer to the opposite door sent me back to Tobias's room. I was not about to be caught in a bathroom with a bunch of minors.

Tobias was sitting on the end of his bed, arms propped on his knees, looking through his phone. I really hadn't seen him on his phone very much, so that was a little jarring. A part of me wanted to know what he was looking at.

I pulled the door shut and clicked the lock.

That got his attention. He tossed the phone over his shoulder like it meant nothing to him. And waited. Again with the waiting.

That was okay. Because I was a hot bitch who knew what she wanted. I didn't need a man making the first moves.

I sucked in a breath.

"We can just go to dinner," he said.

"Fuck dinner."

I approached with confidence, not haste, keeping eye contact the whole time so I could see the slow shifting of emotions across his face.

His tongue darted out to lick across his bottom lip.

I didn't stop until I was wedged firmly between his thighs. His hands slid across my hips and grasped the back of my thighs, fingers perilously close to slipping between them.

"Damn these jeans," he rasped.

In this position, his head was level with my chest, and his hot breath danced over the tops of my breasts. My nipples hardened in response.

I ran my fingers across his forehead and into his hair, tucking it behind his ear.

"You're really pretty." Dammit, I had turned into a blithering idiot by one guy who was ever so slightly more attractive than your average guy.

He just chuckled. "You're really pretty too."

His hands were coming back up my thighs and under my top. When they touched skin, my breath hitched.

I fought the urge to recoil or to stop his hands or to tell him to turn the light off. I usually tried to avoid this part. The inevitable discovery of the belly and back rolls.

But his big hands just skimmed until they brushed against the underside of the hot pink lacy bra I'd worn.

He raised his eyebrows. "Fair is fair."

I didn't protest as he tugged my top up and over my head and discarded it. I shook my hair out.

His hands continued to tease and linger up and around my bra, dancing close to brushing across my nipples, but always stopping short. It was a maddening dance and it was working. Every gentle touch sent a new spark of desire shooting straight down between my thighs.

He pressed a kiss to the top of one of my breasts, beard rasping across the delicate skin, and I sighed, leaning even farther into him.

Finally, his fingers dipped below the top edge of one of the cups, pulling it down until the contents spilled out.

"Careful, these are expensive."

"Your tits or your bra?" He thumbed my exposed nipple and I couldn't stifle my gasp.

"All natural, thank you," I whispered.

"Hmm." He licked over my nipple and suddenly I couldn't give a flying fuck about how much my bra cost. "If I break it, I'll buy you a new one."

The dark tone of his voice made my entire body tighten with anticipation.

Please, baby Jesus, rip the bra to shreds. Rip me to shreds, take me, I don't care.

But then Tobias pulled the whole of my large nipple into his mouth with one strong suck and all thought immediately fled my mind. I was mush. Putty in his mammoth hands.

I could do nothing but hold on to his massive shoulders and groan.

When he removed his hot and wet mouth from my breast, I was bereft and almost complained, but then he kissed me again.

One hand snaked around to my bra clasp and his deft fingers snapped it free in no time. Clever boy.

We were pressed so tightly together, there was no room for the bra to fall, yet. He broke our kiss again so he could remove the bra, clearly frustrated that it'd been keeping him from me. He gathered both heavy breasts into his hands, kneading softly.

"You're magnificent."

The words barely registered through the sultry haze of pleasure and desire thrumming through me.

"Sit on my lap." His hands were pushing at my legs.

Fully lost to the ache at the junction of my thighs, I let him rearrange me so that I was straddling one of his rock-hard thighs.

I didn't have the time or brain space to think about whether I was crushing him or not. Honestly, who cared. The only thing I could concentrate on was the press of his thigh against my pussy, which was also pressed against my panties and my unforgiving jeans.

Oh, fuck.

One hand was on my ass again, one in my hair, and his mouth was again torturing one of my nipples.

My body couldn't resist the stillness any longer and I ground down on his thigh, the sensation oddly satisfying. This seemed to be exactly what he had in mind, because his hand on my ass started pushing, encouraging the grinding.

His mouth sucked, and his tongue licked, and I pressed myself down along the length of his thigh again and again, feeling the pressure build.

This was it. I was going to fucking cream my pants like an overeager and underexperienced teenager.

His teeth on my sensitive nipple was the final straw.

I moaned out my orgasm as I rode his thigh.

He held me as I came down, face pressed into the curve of my neck. I was trembling and flushed. His lips kissed gently up my throat. He had to be feeling the furious pounding of my heartbeat.

"Well." My voice came out raspy and thick, like I'd been screaming. And maybe I had been. Who really knows? "That was..." I couldn't even find a word to describe it. Shameful, me being a journalism major and all. I felt like "fucking awesome" would inflate his ego a bit much. But the man had made me orgasm and had barely touched me and I didn't really know what to do with that information.

"Are you okay, though?" I attempted to get up, but both my legs were made of jelly.

Ever the gentleman, Tobias helped me plop facedown on his bed. The supine position was a good one for me because it hid my belly and accentuated my ass. I adjusted the girls to make myself a little more comfortable, and propped my chin on my hands.

Tobias stretched out beside me, body angled towards mine.

"But, really, I didn't squish you?"

His eyes sparkled. "If that's the way I go, that's just the way I go." He brushed a thick lock of hair away from my face. "But, really, I'm fine."

That's when I remembered. My orgasm-riddled brain had totally forgotten that I was conveniently the only one who received an orgasm. *Whoops.*

Judging by the tight bulge in the front of Tobias's painted-on jeans, I wouldn't have to work particularly hard.

I reached for the front of his jeans, but he stopped me.

"Fair is fair," I said.

"Touché. But I like that this was about you. A little blue balls never killed anyone. I'll live."

"Are you sure?" That was new. I was usually the one who had to go home with blue balls.

He leaned in and kissed my forehead. "Next time."

"Oh, there'll be a next time?"

"Jesus, I hope so, or I just threw away my shot." He grinned. "Hungry?"

You know what, I was suddenly ravenous.

We walked to the deli that was close to campus for sustenance. Tobias's treat, again. I had to avoid Tanner's eyes both coming and going, because I'm pretty sure he would be able to read what we had been doing all over my face.

I just gave him cursory waves.

On the way back, he hollered a friendly, "Have a good night, guys."

That got me thinking as I cradled my club sandwich. The time was creeping past eleven. I had already told Amera not to wait up, but I hadn't really planned on being out that late. The later it got, the more questions arose about possible sleeping arrangements. A topic of conversation that hadn't been broached yet. I would hate to eat and run, but I kind of liked the idea of leaving him wanting more.

We had made it back to Tobias's room before I finished all my mental dithering.

Guess I was eating, then.

We posted up at the end of his bed, picnic-style. He was gracious enough to let me use the desk chair and a lap desk so I could pick at my sandwich, pretending to eat it. Some habits die hard.

Tobias didn't have any qualms about his appetite. He'd gotten a double meat, double cheese, veggie loaded monstrosity and consumed it with the same vigor that he did...other things.

I pulled pieces off mine and set them in my mouth delicately, so as not to drop anything on my cleavage. Although, I'm not sure he would mind that much.

"So," I said, "what happened with your ex-girlfriend?"

He choked.

"Sorry. Too soon?"

"No." He cleared his throat. "Honestly surprised you waited this long to ask."

"Well, I was previously...preoccupied." He grinned his sly wolf grin and I felt my face flush. Ugh. But I continued. "Now I can turn my attention to other things."

"So it's not really what you're thinking."

"And how would you know what I'm thinking?"

"Cause I've had this conversation before."

I frowned. "I thought you said I was the first girl you've brought up here."

"I do also have conversations in places that are not my bedroom."

"Fair enough. Proceed."

"It's not even an exciting story. It was mutual. We had just outgrown each other. Are you the same person you were at sixteen?"

God, I hoped not. I spent a whole hell of a lot of time trying not to be that person anymore.

"That's it?"

"Yup. We had barely spoken to each other in weeks, and hadn't seen each other in person for months. She called me up one day and I considered letting it go to voicemail. I should have been excited to talk to her, you know? Especially after so long. But I literally dreaded it. That's when I knew something had to change. She came up for a few days, but we couldn't work it out. The end." He took another huge bite of his sandwich, completely unaffected by the telling of the tale. I supposed I should be happy that he wasn't hung up on some other girl.

"But still. Six years is a long time."

He shrugged. "It was good, and now it's over. I think I learned and grew a lot. It's exciting to see what else is out there."

He wiggled his eyebrows at me in what I'm sure he thought was a suggestive invitation, but all it did was send a shiver of unease down my spine. He was excited to see what else was out there. Which confirmed my earlier suspicions that he wasn't looking for anything serious. He was looking for rebound sex. Not that I had never been rebound sex or had never had rebound sex.

I had to rebound after every time I dealt with Justin, the sooner the better, usually. Wasn't that why I said yes to Tobias in the first place?

I still couldn't help the disappointment that broiled in my stomach, though. I had found the flaw. And I was desperately hoping Tobias would be the unicorn.

I made a show of yawning aggressively. I looked at my phone. "Hey, it's getting late."

He was staring at me, forehead furrowed in consternation. I made a show of tidying up my trash and studiously avoided meeting his eyes. He looked like he wanted to say something. I wanted him to say something, anything, to change my mind.

"Can I walk you home?"

Meh, not really what I was expecting.

But I nodded.

It was only a ten-minute walk to our house, which was another perk of the location. It meant I could still walk to all my classes without needing a car.

Amera had left the porch light on for me.

"Well, good night."

He grabbed my arm. "Bryn, wait." I turned to face him again. "I had a good time tonight. I hope I get to see you again."

Was he really that oblivious? I thought about the kinds of letters I got for my column. About the kinds of shenanigans the guys at this damn school pulled. Yes, he was really that oblivious. I could imagine the letter I would write in this situation.

Dear Bryn, the guy I really like, but have only been out with twice, but made me orgasm with the force of a tycoon without even touching my lady bits, just told me he wasn't looking for anything serious. What to do?

What to do, indeed.

"Yeah, sure, just text me. I might be busy with work, but I'll let you know." There. Two of us could play the casual, noncommittal game. I could be a cool girl.

His pretty face was pulled into a frown that was not really a frown...yet. I had the feeling that he was deliberately trying to keep his expression neutral. And here I just wanted him to be honest. Was that really so much to ask for?

So be it.

I gave him the perfunctory smile and wave I'd given Tanner, and flounced up the porch steps, not looking back.

CHAPTER EIGHT

THE WRONG SWIPE

Dear Bryn,

A few months ago, I started a friends-with-benefits arrangement with a guy I met in biology. We both agreed on the boundaries of our relationship. Here's the thing, though: I really like him! He's smart and funny and I enjoy spending time with him outside of just the benefits.

What do I do?

Caught Feelings

Hello, Caught!

So, you have unfortunately fallen into one of the pitfalls of the friends-with-benefits situation. Inevitably, one side usually catches feelings for the other. That's what makes friends-with-benefits such a fraught endeavor and why I always advise that you choose your FWB partners carefully. Sex muddies and complicates our relationships, even if we try to convince ourselves otherwise.

You don't want to go into a FWB hoping that your partner is going to eventually change their mind and want a different kind of relationship. That's unfair to them and is going to mean heartbreak and misery for you.

That doesn't sound like what you've done here, but the feelings have happened anyway. Here's what you do now: tell your FWB immediately. You do not want to keep the status quo and hope he just realizes he also has feelings. You are 100% going to get hurt if you pretend nothing is different.

Here's a script:

Hey, sex friend, I've realized my feelings have changed since we started hooking up. I'm going to need to stop. I'd love to stay just friends and see how that goes! (Only add this if it's true. You have to be okay with being just friends. Again, don't go into the friend relationship either hoping he might change his mind. That's manipulative.)

You've now left the ball in his court! His response might surprise you.

Good luck!

Chapter Nine

I AM NO LONGER NAKED

The part about me being busy with work was a total lie. I worked four-or five-hour shifts, at the most.

To his credit, Tobias did not go radio silent. We texted, he asked me about my day, I asked him about his plants, he sent me pictures of Twix and Milk Dud with their new forever families.

I tried not to be too disappointed when the third day passed and he still hadn't asked to hang out again. Clearly, he had picked up on my distance the last time we saw each other.

Stupid girl.

You wanted him before, damn the consequences, so what's the difference.

The difference, self, is that it's different when they actually say the words out loud. It's different when you know they just want casual sex. Ignorance is bliss and all that.

Tobias didn't actually say that, though.

It's exciting to see what else is out there, is what he said.

Didn't exactly inspire a picture of monogamy. Is that what I wanted, though? To be monogamous? The Wrong Swipe girl finally gets a boyfriend. There is actually hope for everyone.

Boyfriend. The dreaded and yet elusive B word. Why was I thinking about the B word after only two dates?

Because if anyone was made of boyfriend material, it'd be Tobias-freaking-puppies-Doan.

On one of my extra breaks at work, I watched in real time as Tobias posted pictures to his Instagram stories of some kind of special bonding activity he and the high school babies were doing.

Leaning against the espresso machine I was supposed to be manning, I blew out a huff of air. WHY DID HE HAVE TO BE SO HOT AND PHILANTHROPIC?

He could be hot or he could be philanthropic. Being both was definitely too much.

Ugh. Why did I *care*? Because I had broken the cardinal rules of dating: I had let one good orgasm completely rattle my brain and destroy my critical-thinking skills. I had become attached to the high of stomach butterflies.

Tobias had done nothing wrong.

I was just irrational.

Just as I was about to open the messenger app, Tobias's number popped up on my phone. *Oh, fuck.* He was calling me. I had summoned him by the sheer force of my overthinking.

I let it ring a few times, just to make him think I wasn't waiting by the phone.

"Hello?"

"I only have about five minutes, but I know I said something wrong and I need you to tell me what it was so I can fix it."

"Oh, uh."

My first instinct was to babble a quick "nothing, everything is totally fine, why do you ask?" But I knew why he was asking. Because I couldn't hold my shit together and acted like a weirdo. My first impression of Tobias was that he's honest, not a game player. So, what would happen if I was honest too?

"So, um...I was just a little thrown when you said you wanted to see what else is out there after...um, we, you know." Sometimes I was just so articulate.

There was a significant pause on his end where I tried not to breathe too heavily into the phone.

"I don't date more than one person at a time." Pause pause pause. "That being said, I want to see you again."

The giddy rush of endorphins to my system almost made me black out. "Yes. Yes, I would like that too." I tried not to sound too excited, but I think I failed at that endeavor.

"Good. Tonight. I'll text you."

And then he was gone.

I exhaled a sigh of relief. I hadn't fucked things up beyond repair after all. And the way he had barked *good* into my ear had my toes tingling.

Tobias had to wait for Tanner to relieve him for the night shift, which meant he wasn't available until almost nine again.

I used the free time to speed clean the house the best I could after my shift. I was not a natural housekeeper, and neither was

Amera, which meant we usually ended up with stacks of weird clutter everywhere. Bras hanging off the kitchen chairs? How did those get there? We never knew.

Amera had gone to her not-boyfriend's house for the weekend, which relieved some of the pressure from Tobias coming over to our house. I didn't know if I was ready to start introducing him to my friends yet.

Amera being gone also meant that I was on my own for outfit selection.

It took me almost two hours to decide on a pair of leggings and a long tunic, but it was what was under the leggings that really mattered.

I toyed with the idea of answering the door in some barely-there lingerie, but that would mean I assumed we were definitely having sex. And while I was pretty sure we were definitely having sex, I didn't want him to know that. It's complicated, I know.

Under my clothes, I donned a burgundy lace bodysuit, cut high on my hips and low down the front. The girls were barely contained in unlined cups and rested mostly in their natural position. It was easy on, easy off, with just a hook and eye closure, and could be removed in one fell swoop.

The thong back chafed a bit, so I was kinda counting on Tobias removing it rather quickly. Beauty is pain, after all.

A text came in at 9:05 from Tobias.

Omw

There were those fucking butterflies again, lighting up my insides like they had a right to be there.

I was fluffing my hair one more time when the doorbell rang; I had taken the time to straighten it, so the mermaid vibes were strong.

I swung the door open and was suddenly very glad I was fully clothed.

"I brought pasta!" Tobias said cheerily, holding up a bag of takeout from Beppe's. How did he know pasta was one of my favorite food groups?

Yes, very glad I had all my clothes on so that I was ready to eat some pasta.

Tobias had stepped up his outfit game. He had on a pair of relaxed-fit, khaki-colored pants, a shiny pair of leather, lace-up boots, and a maroon Henley that casually had the sleeves rolled up. I could see the outline of his chest under the Henley. *Goddammit.*

His hair was down and wavy, curling gently over his shoulders.

I smiled and held the door open; he brushed past me in a miasma of expensive-smelling cologne and pasta. Yum.

He set the bag on the kitchen table to gather me in a hug. I was engulfed by his arms and chest, which was saying something. I took the opportunity to bury my nose in his chest, conveniently right between his cut pectorals.

His hands skimmed my ribs and stomach as we pulled apart and I could tell by the look on his face that he could feel the lacy bodysuit under my tunic.

"Are you providing dessert?"

"Wouldn't you like to know."

His eyes sparkled. "I would."

I sashayed to the cutlery drawer and found two forks and grabbed two mismatched plates from the cabinet.

Tobias was sitting and dishing out food.

"I didn't know what you would like, so I just ordered you my favorite."

I had a split second of fear—thinking that he'd just brought us salads or something dumb—but I shouldn't have worried.

There were two side salads, yes, but also two large containers of pasta. I joined him at the table while Tobias opened our food.

"Fettuccine Beppe," he said with a smile.

Fettuccine Beppe was fettuccine alfredo with grilled chicken, peas, and mushrooms. It looked and smelled divine.

Tobias had also gotten us both Caesar salads and a loaf of crunchy bread that was still warm. The man knew the way to a girl's heart with alarming precision.

As we ate, we chatted about small, everyday things. I asked him what he was doing with the high schoolers today and he explained their team-building activities and what kind of programs they were doing at Penn Warren.

I told him a little bit about Amera and Sebastian and how we had clicked together freshman year. He complimented the house and I told him about Amera's parents' connections.

During a quick lull in the conversation, I asked him when his birthday was.

He looked momentarily startled before answering. "January fourth."

"You're a Capricorn."

Well, that made complete and utter sense. Caps were practical, realistic, persistent, and disciplined. They also tended to have strong control over their urges and desires. Which explained a whole hell of a lot.

"How did you just know that? Off the top of your head?"

I toyed with a swirl of noodles on my plate. "Um, I like astrology, specifically horoscopes." I held out my arm, wrist-up, so he could see the bull's head tattooed on the inside of my wrist. "Taurus." Gentle and fierce; built for comfort and pleasure; loyal.

He gave a little laugh. "Yeah, I saw that. I thought maybe you just liked cows."

I flushed. "It is not a cow. It is a bull."

He held his hands up in supplication, humor still written all over his face. "I apologize." He grabbed my arm and brought it to his mouth, lips moving lazily over my tattoo. "I like the bull very much."

Suddenly, the room was too hot. Suddenly, all the air was gone from my lungs.

I wanted to make him come undone, like he'd done to me. I wanted to watch his face break apart under my fingers.

I stood up so abruptly from the table, that I sent my chair skittering. Tobias did the same, albeit with more grace and subtlety.

Neither of us said anything, but I could feel his eyes on me as I led him to my boudoir. I had preemptively set up my room, so I didn't have to worry about it in the moment. Candles were lit, the pink globs in my lava lamp danced merrily, and I had strung a line of twinkle lights above the headboard.

I worked better in the dark. Felt more confident and full of myself, knowing he wouldn't be able to see every nook and cranny and flaw and hair out of place in bright light.

The door clicked shut behind me.

I whirled around, pulse hammering in my ears, to find Tobias leaning casually against the closed door.

Another plus of the dimness: I couldn't see his eyes. But I knew they were there, his eerily intense stare boring into my body.

We stepped forward in unison and I knew what was coming: the kiss. I sunk into his embrace the second our lips met. It felt just so damn good.

The kiss was hot and urgent and hungry. It was the kiss of a desperate man. And, hey, I couldn't say I wasn't a little desperate myself.

He tugged my shirt over my head, discarded it on the floor.

His big hands skimmed over the lace of my skimpy outfit. He brushed across my nipples and they immediately hardened into sharp, eager peaks. Traitors.

I grabbed his wrists and could feel the pulse hammering there. "No, tonight it's my turn."

That wolf smile flashed. "I am yours to command." The husky smolder of his voice sent chills rippling across my skin.

"Take your clothes off."

Tobias shed his clothes expertly and expediently, while I shucked off my leggings so he could witness the rest of the bodysuit.

All that was left was his tight boxer briefs.

All the air left my lungs in one swish.

He was magnificent. Tobias Doan did not skip leg day; the bottom half was just as sculpted as the top half.

Man legs usually weren't my cup of tea, but I could make an exception. His jeans were hiding nothing.

He ran a finger down the exposed flesh between my breasts, but I didn't let him get any further.

"Get on the bed."

"I like where this is going." His tone was playful.

I liked that about him, that he could swing from sexpot to playful and back again. It made me feel like he didn't take himself so seriously. That he was fun and that sex could be fun. And it was fun, usually, but could also be so serious. I wanted it to be fun.

He sprawled on my bed, head propped on some decorative pillows, arms stacked behind his head. He was too big for my bed, but I guess we would have to make do.

The annoying boxer briefs were still on.

I guessed I would have to take care of those myself. I climbed up on the bed—trying not to pay attention to how much it dipped—and settled myself between those massive thighs.

Heat radiated off his body in waves.

I took a steadying breath that I hoped wasn't too obvious and ran my nails down from hip to knee. His skin seemed to pulsate under my touch.

The bulge hidden beneath his boxer briefs grew considerably.

I repeated the movements, inching perilously close to his waistband. I could tell he was trying to remain calm and unaffected, but was gallantly failing. His breathing had quickened, and his muscles were pulled into hard lines.

I smiled. This was the fun part.

I leaned down and pressed a wet kiss to the contour of his shaft and was rewarded with a strained, "Fuck."

Tobias didn't strike me as the kind of guy who used expletives a lot, so the F-bomb coming from his sweet mouth was particularly titillating.

It was time to put him out of his misery.

I slipped my fingers into the waistband of his boxer briefs and tugged; Tobias eagerly lifted his hips to help with the unveiling.

I let a small huff escape my mouth.

"Well done, sir."

He laughed.

Now, let's be honest: penises, in general, were not a very attractive part of the male anatomy. There's an evolutionary reason why the penis is on a part of the body that can conveniently be hidden by clothing. We have to be lured in by a pretty face or a good personality so that we can accept the funky penis. The penis was built for fun and functionality and not for looks. Which is why it always baffled me when they would hit us with the unsolicited dick pic. Like, get that hairy, weird and bumpy, slightly curved thing away from me before I even know if I *like* you.

I would say Tobias was the exception. He had a pretty penis. He also appeared to be a manscaper, which was much appreciated. He was well-proportioned to the size of his body.

I ran a nail down the side of the taut shaft; it was warm to the touch.

"Jesus Christ, Bryn."

I circled the shaft with my whole hand and began pumping in a steady rhythm. I wasn't sure if his cock could get thicker, but apparently it could, and did so under my hand.

I slid my tongue over the soft and sensitive head of his cock, teasing, before taking the whole of him into my mouth.

He moaned in agony and thrust his hips up as I took him deeper into my throat. I slid a hand under his body to sink my nails into one of his rounded ass cheeks. I deepened my sucking and that drove him crazy. His hips pumped in time with the movement of my mouth.

His hand had found its way to my hair, tangling in the long strands, but I didn't need any guidance. He wasn't pushy, though, only needed something to hold on to.

"Oh, fuck, Bryn." The hand in my hair tightened. "I'm going to come."

I pulled my mouth off him for just a second. "Do it."

He groaned, breath coming in heaves. "Are you sure?"

My answer was to suck him back into my mouth, adding my hand again to the pumping.

With a deep and relieved growling sound, Tobias ground out his orgasm into my throat. I swallowed everything he gave me.

Almost immediately he had pulled himself to a sitting position and grabbed my face in his hands, lips coming to mine. There was something deliciously erotic about the way he kissed me now, languid and leisurely, his tongue sliding across my lips. Could he taste himself there?

After the kiss, he plopped back down on the pillows with a sated sigh. He was only partially soft, so I imagine it wouldn't take him long to revv back up, but I could give the guy a break for a minute. Even though I was positively throbbing with want for him.

I climbed in beside him, wedging myself under his arm, head on his chest and one leg thrown over his.

It was nice, our bodies tucked together. Almost too nice.

Tobias sighed again and his eyes were closed, long lashes lying softly on his cheeks. This fucker better not be falling asleep. I wasn't even sure if I wanted him to spend the night yet or not.

I needn't have worried because Tobias was talking again soon enough.

"No family pictures?"

My head popped up to look at his serene face. "What?"

He nodded towards the nightstand.

Oh.

I had several framed pictures there: me and Sheenah, a group picture from senior prom which included about six people I didn't talk to anymore, some of Amera, Bastian, and me, and then one of me and Justin. We were standing in front of a sink, both looking over our shoulders at the picture-taker. It was from the senior chili fundraiser and we hadn't arrived together, just happened to be working together at the same time, conveniently for the picture. It was the only one we had together because Justin didn't do pictures.

I felt a tingle of guilt, lying here with Tobias but thinking about Justin.

But that's not what Tobias had asked about. He'd asked about my family.

"Um, yeah. Our relationship is...tumultuous."

He nodded like he understood. Did his mom think he was a fat slut too? Doubt it.

"Yeah, my dad is getting remarried this year."

Well, maybe he did have some experience with parental baggage.

"I assume you're not happy about that?"

He shrugged, or shrugged as much as he could with me lying on one of his arms. "My mom and dad have been divorced for years. And Dad has been dating this woman for years. I know her. I even like her. But it's different, you know, when they start making it official. Like, now they're really never getting back together. It's so final."

"What about your mom?"

"She's okay. But I think it feels too final for her too. She would never admit this, but I think she was always holding out hope that they'd get back together."

"Was the divorce not mutual?"

"Irreconcilable differences, as they say. They just didn't mesh well together when I was a kid. I think Mom was expecting to reconcile when I got old enough to take care of myself. And then Margot came along, and there went that plan."

"Is she sad, your mom?"

"She'll never admit it, but I think so. I'm kinda hoping once the wedding happens, that she'll finally move on and find someone that makes her happy."

"Mm-hmm."

He poked me in the ribs. "What about your story? I've told mine."

"That wasn't much of a story. You seem pretty well adjusted." I was drawing whorls in the downy hair of his abdomen.

"Well, I spent a lot of time talking about it in therapy when I was in high school, so I've had a lot of processing time."

What must that feel like? To have parents that supported your need to process your shit. Tobias was so open, it was startling. There was no guile there, no mincing of words, no long pauses as he thought of the best thing to say to get the desired outcome. Was this what it felt like when someone was telling the truth?

I was about to open my mouth to tell him about my shit, but then I heard the front door rattling, then crashing open, then a voice, "BRYN, I'M HOME. YOU BETTER NOT BE NAKED IN THE COMMON AREAS AGAIN."

I started so hard I almost knocked Tobias off the bed. "Shit."

He rolled off and grabbed the first piece of clothing he could reach—my shirt—and held it up to his chest like that was going to do anything. "Do I need to go out the window?"

I choked on a laugh. "No, hold on."

I slid off the bed and grabbed a cotton bathrobe from the back of the closet door. "Wait here."

I left Tobias in the safety of my room and went to find Amera flinging her purse into a chair and then plopping onto the couch.

I made sure the sash of my robe was cinched tight. "What are you doing here? I thought you were spending the weekend at Elliot's?"

Her gaze turned towards me and I noticed the puffy eyelids and the smeared mascara. Shit. I tried not to glance back towards my room because that would one hundred percent make me a shitty friend.

Amera's eyes raked me from tousled hair to naked toes. She grinned. "Have you been busy?"

I pulled the robe a little tighter. "Maybe."

Her voice lowered to a theatrical whisper. "Have you guys had sex yet?"

I gave her a wide-eyed, shut-up look. "No." This time I did glance back, just to make sure the door was still closed and Tobias hadn't wandered out. "Are you okay, Mer?"

She grabbed one of the couch pillows and hugged it to her chest, curling her legs up on the couch, where Odafin quickly joined her, since he had been locked out of my room.

She scratched at his ears absently. "Nothing I can't handle."

Amera claimed that Elliot wasn't really her boyfriend, but that apparently didn't stop him from making her upset about something. Not that she would admit that.

"Are you sure?"

She eyed my robe again. "I am not having this conversation with you, who is obviously naked."

"Oh." I flushed. "Right. Almost forgot about that part."

She waved me off, grabbing the remote. "Go back to your man and enjoy."

When I got back to my room, I found Tobias curled under my floral comforter, hands tucked up under his chin. He was, for all appearances, dead-ass asleep and snoring softly. His hair spilled across the pillows like a Disney princess.

He appeared to have tried to leave room for me, but there was no way I was fitting in the small space of bed he managed to leave between his giant torso and giant legs.

I found a comfy pair of pajama pants and an old T-shirt.

Grabbing an extra pillow and blanket, I headed back to the living room.

Amera had wrapped herself in large, fluffy blanket in my absence and found an old action movie on regular TV.

She looked up when I curled up on the opposite end of the couch. "That was alarmingly quick."

I sighed. "He's asleep."

She laughed. "Sorry for the cockblock."

"I'll live." I leaned my head on the back of the couch. "I now have free time to talk about Elliot. And, as you can see, I am no longer naked."

She started threading braids through her fingers. Which I knew was a tell that she didn't want anyone to know was a tell. "Nothing, really. He told me he wanted to be exclusive and I told him I didn't have time for boyfriends, and he told me he didn't have time to waste, and then I left."

Only Amera would be put out that a man wanted to be exclusive. "And that made you upset?"

"I will not be given an ultimatum." Her phone buzzed where it was propped on her knee. She thumbed through what appeared to be a very long text. "Right on time. My apology." She held it out for me to inspect, and it was, indeed, a paragraph from Elliot, begging for her forgiveness.

"Girl, you need to tell me your secrets."

"No secrets." She stuffed the phone into the cushions without replying. "My dad started my car for me every day before high school. He'd probably still be doing it if I lived closer." She snuggled down into the pillows and blankets. "If that tells you anything about how I expect to be treated by men."

My heart twinged painfully, as it usually did whenever Amera mentioned her doting and over-involved parents, especially her dad. I had been without mine for almost ten years, but an ache, a void, like that never really goes away. If he were still alive, I'd like to think he would be doting, over-involved, starting my car, moving me into my freshman dorm and wiping his brow with a kerchief he kept in the back pocket of his light wash jeans.

In the summers, he would sneak us popsicles, even after Mom had said no. We'd always be caught with stained lips and sticky fingers. Mom would frown and then Dad would kiss her cheek with his artificial blue lips and she'd smile and soften. She was gentler in those days, more forgiving of all our faults.

CHAPTER TEN

TOO HOT TO BE TRUSTED

I awoke slowly to the sizzling of bacon and murmur of voices. It was nice and cozy until I recognized Amera's tinkling bell laugh and Tobias's low rumble.

I instantly froze, muscles tensing up under the blanket, my fight-or-flight reflexes kicking into high gear.

In my blissful sleep-state, I had forgotten I'd left Tobias all alone in my room last night.

Shit, shit, shit.

I tried sinking deeper into the pillow, covertly tugging the blanket over my face. Maybe they wouldn't notice. Maybe Tobias would just leave and we wouldn't have to do the morning-after dance that I wasn't prepared for.

"Bryn, your new special friend is delightful," Amera said.

Ah, fuck.

I sat up, feigning a pretend yawn like I'd just woken up. "Oh, you guys are awake already."

Amera gave me a look. "It's ten o'clock."

I grabbed my phone off the coffee table. So it was. "Oh, fuck." I threw the blanket off. "My shift is at eleven."

Tobias had this cute, bemused expression on his face. His hair was sexily tousled, while I was sure mine looked like a haphazard rat's nest. I tried to pat things down and rub smeared makeup off. This was not how I imagined our first morning together would go.

He held up two plates of eggs, toast, and bacon. "But I made breakfast."

I dawdled with indecision. "I have to pee, then shower, then, uh...work."

I threw finger guns as I slunk away to the bathroom. FINGER GUNS. Finger. Guns. At my back, I heard Amera say, "I'll take breakfast."

I dilly-dallied long enough in the shower that I was almost one hundred percent sure I'd be late to work and that Tobias couldn't have possibly waited around that long.

10:35.

I pulled my wet hair into a messy bun and slapped on some basic makeup so I looked halfway presentable.

Amera was sitting at the kitchen table next to two dirty plates. Her long legs were crossed and she looked up at me from the top of her glasses. She'd been waiting.

I slung my purse over my shoulder and attempted a hasty exit. "See ya later!"

"Excuse me. What the hell was that?"

I froze and deflated. "I don't know."

"Well, you better figure it out because you're gonna scare him away if you don't stop acting ridiculous."

Amera's pronouncement consumed me so much I didn't even have a snide remark ready when Ethan chided me for being late.

I just apologized and headed for the time clock which really threw him for a loop. He stared after me, slack-jawed.

Amera was right, unfortunately. I was acting erratic, full of contradictions and indecision, and not like the cool girl. As much as Tobias set off fireworks in my lady bits, he also set off alarm bells in my head.

Wasn't it every girl's dream to wake up with a hot guy in her bed? Not me, not yet. He wasn't supposed to see morning-after me this early. Waking up together felt a lot more intimate than just sex, and I was still holding him at arm's length.

Tobias was too hot to be trusted.

I knew it, but I didn't want to know it.

I had been at this game long enough. I knew what my league was, and knew when I was batting above it. So I needed to decide if I was going to risk swinging or not.

Ugh, sports analogies.

Almost two uneventful hours went by while I was lost in my thoughts and wordless café music. I almost dropped a stack of books when I heard his voice.

"Ethan, hey, man."

"Toby, bro, good to see you again."

I heard them shaking, or smacking, hands, or whatever dude-bros do. I stayed hidden in the nonfiction.

"Can I get one green tea and one iced white mocha?"

Yum, white mocha, my favorite.

Oh, shit.

I quickly stuffed books on the appropriate shelves and patted down my slightly wavy, slightly crunchy, air-dried hair.

Was that supposed to be for me? Unless Tobias was in my place of employment buying a basic coffee for some other basic white girl. Which was totally possible.

His voice rose an octave higher. "Bryn St. Jean, I know you're in here."

Emerging from the stacks, I feigned surprise to see him. "Tobias!"

He already had his tea, and the machines whirred as Ethan made my drink. Tobias was wearing tight-ass athletic leggings and one of those slick, moisture-wicking shirts. He might as well have been fucking naked for all intents and purposes. I could see every contour.

Fuck.

He smiled when he saw me. Ethan handed him my drink.

"You didn't eat breakfast."

Slightly red-faced, I looked at Ethan and said, "I'm going to take my break now, cool?"

Ethan looked for a second like he was about to argue, but there was literally no one else in the bookstore. And I guess he liked us both enough to be lenient. "Just your fifteen, okay."

Tobias tipped his cup. "Thanks, man."

There were only a few tables in the café area, but I really didn't relish the idea of Ethan overhearing whatever conversation Tobias and I were about to have. There were other tables spread through the store, so I led Tobias to the one farthest from the café and entrance.

Tobias handed me my drink and I took a sip gratefully. The sugar wouldn't sit well on an empty stomach, but who cared. The caffeine was sorely needed.

Tobias watched me over the rim of his cup, his expression reminding me eerily of Amera earlier this morning.

Great.

So we were going to talk.

Decide, decide.

To stall some more, I pulled my phone out of my apron pocket and slid it onto the table so I could keep track of the time.

"So, listen. I'm not a morning person."

He laughed. "No kidding."

"I was...kind of a mess."

He gave a sort of noncommittal grunt and took a sip of his tea. I guess I was going to have to lead this conversation. After all, I had basically fled at the sight of him in my kitchen. And Tobias still hadn't done anything wrong and I was treating him like some sort of vicious monster who would bite my head off at the first sign of vulnerability.

The little voice in the back of my mind said, *but he could do worse*.

We each stalled by taking sips of our drinks at alternating intervals.

"I'm sorry," I said finally.

"I would have left if you asked."

"I know, but you were already asleep. I try not to be that big of a bitch."

"Your tiny bed wasn't exactly comfortable. I wouldn't have minded." He stretched languidly in his chair and I felt a rush of heat go to my face...and other places.

Nicely played, Mr. Doan.

Suddenly, the table started vibrating as my phone buzzed. Shaw black heart emoji popped up on the screen as an incoming call.

My stomach bottomed out. I hit the power button with haste.

If Tobias noticed anything amiss, he didn't acknowledge it. Which I greatly appreciated, as I didn't know what I would say if he asked about Justin right now.

I held up my cup. "Thanks for the coffee, though. It was needed."

The table buzzed again and my phone moved in a lazy circle with the incoming call. This time Tobias did notice.

"Do you need to get that?"

My jaw clenched and I snatched the phone off the table. "Yeah, just give me a minute."

I hustled to the stockroom, which I hoped was far enough out of hearing range. I picked up the third call.

"What do you need?"

"Nice to hear from you too, baby girl."

His throaty voice slid through me like honey. I hadn't heard from him since the day he drove all the way up here for apparently nothing from me.

"I'm at work. I can't really talk."

"Okay, hey, I need your help."

I slouched against the wall, closing my eyes, like that would somehow help. That if my eyes were closed, I somehow couldn't see myself doing this. Again.

"What do you need?"

"Can you wire me some cash?"

"How much?"

"Not a lot, a few hundred."

I exhaled. "Justin. I don't have a few hundred dollars."

I mean, theoretically, I could pull together three hundred dollars from a few different accounts. But I had bills to pay, rent, my internship application fee, and I needed to save up for the semester since I wasn't able to work as many hours at The Bookery once school started again.

"Really anything would help, please, I really need this." The inflection of his voice had changed. He almost sounded panicky. It tugged at my gut like it always did.

"I'll see what I can do. But it won't be till I get off."

I almost hoped the delay would get me off the hook.

It didn't.

"You're the best, baby girl. I knew I could count on you. I don't know what I would do without you, Vivi."

I thought about what I told Tobias last night about my star sign, Taurus. Dependable, reliable. Loyal.

"Text me the details."

"Already sent. Catch you later, baby girl."

And then he was gone. And, indeed, I already had a text message.

Sliding the phone back into my apron, I hurried back to our table, but Tobias was gone.

Ah, fuck.

I made a beeline for the front door. Maybe he hadn't gotten far and I could catch him if I hurried.

Ethan looked startled when I busted through the front door, sending the overhead bell tinkling like mad.

There he was, almost to the bus stop.

"Tobias! Tobias, wait!" My voice was high-pitched and shrill, but effective. He stopped and turned around. I saw a moment of hesitation, but then he started walking briskly back towards me.

I waited on the sidewalk in front of the bookstore, trying to calm the frantic racing of my heart.

Tobias didn't stop until there were only inches separating our bodies and I had to tilt my head to look up into his face. Which did nothing for my pulse.

"I want this," I said.

"What's this?"

I waved my arms wildly. "Whatever. Whatever this is. Whatever you want."

His eyes were smoldering. He cupped my chin with one hand. "What do you want?"

I had to inhale deeply before responding. And it came out barely a whisper. "You."

Fuck everything. Fuck everyone. Fuck Shaw, fuck leagues, fuck baseball bats, fuck caution, fuck everything I knew about hot boys, fuck everything my mother had ever said about what kinds of guys would want me.

I was fucking swinging.

CHAPTER ELEVEN

TOBIAS, JESUS CHRIST

Tobias and I spent the next few weeks going out on platonic dates. Well, sort of platonic. There was a lot of kissing. A lot. And heavy petting when the setting allowed.

We did the best we could with our work schedules. I worked at The Bookery for ten straight days to try to make up the money I'd wired Justin.

I actually wasn't as bad off as I thought I'd be. Unbeknownst to me, my mom had put five hundred dollars in my bank account on my birthday. She apparently did that instead of calling me. I took the extra hours anyway because I hated having to rely on her for money. I mainly used her money for textbooks and other school expenses. She gave me so much money to assuage her guilt for being a horrible mother.

Tobias had to take most of the night shifts at the dorm because Tanner had a family emergency.

It was quite frankly torture.

The sexual tension swelled between us like an over-inflated balloon. About to burst.

I wanted him more than I had wanted anyone in my life. I could only go so far with my imagination and little vibrator and his increasingly saucy texts were not helping anything.

On Friday night, I got a text.

One of my favorite indies is playing tomorrow night. Come with?

Yes

Tobias was picking me up at eight.

I didn't know what kind of vehicle we were driving in, but he had managed to obtain one. It would be nice not to have to take the bus or Uber. The band was conveniently playing at Club 452.

Not knowing exactly what one wore to these kinds of events, I just dressed to look hot. I wore a boxy, black, mesh see-through dress with a tight black sheath underneath and wedged sneakers.

The wedges would be killing me by the end of the night, but they made my ass and legs look great, so sacrifices had to be made.

Tobias showed up right on time in a midsize sedan and I could immediately tell that he wasn't the one driving. The person on the driver's side was significantly shorter. And appeared to have breasts.

My heart stopped. My mind flipped immediately to the worst-case scenario: he had brought another girl on our date. Even worse, this was not our date, this was *their* date, and I was the other woman. But that made literally zero sense. Also but, sometimes boys made literally zero sense. But but again, Bryn of The Wrong Swipe didn't believe in coincidences and out of thin air and didn't see it coming. There was always a reason. Always a motivation.

I was frozen in place on the sidewalk and Tobias jumped out of the car and loped to greet me.

His hands grazed down my arms before squeezing me in a hug. He was also in all black, so at least I had the dress code down.

He kissed the top of my head. "You look amazing."

"Uhm, thanks." I was super distracted by whomever was still in the driver's seat.

Tobias must have caught my gaze, because he leaned over and knocked on the window.

The window came down and a gorgeous redhead was revealed.

"Y'all get in the car, we're gonna be late!"

Her accent was twangy as fuck, but it suited her cute face. She had long, wavy red hair, that I would bet my life on was natural. As a dye job connoisseur, I could usually spot a good dye job from a bad one. She had effortlessly thick eyebrows and a heavy smattering of freckles across her nose and cheeks. She wore a series of leather cords around a slender neck and black T-shirt with the band's logo. The only makeup was a layer of light eye makeup and clear lip gloss.

"Bryn, this is Emory Storey. Emory, Bryn. Emory is my future stepsister."

The tension immediately fizzled from my body; I felt my shoulders slump.

"Pleasure's all mine, cupcake, now get in the car."

Oh, lord.

Tobias just grinned and went to open the passenger side door for me. I didn't argue. I didn't relish the idea of climbing in and out of the back seat in my outfit.

He popped his head between the seats as Emory peeled away and continued his narration.

"Emory is transferring to Penn Warren this year. What'll you be? A junior?"

"That's right."

That was interesting. That Tobias's dad's new wife had a daughter almost the same age as him, which meant she was probably almost the same age as Tobias's dad. Thus breaking the all too ubiquitous narrative of divorced dudes going for much younger women.

"Emory's also dating Catatonic Divinity's lead guitarist, which is how we scored these tight tickets."

He ruffled her hair with warm familiarity.

She didn't protest. If anyone touched my hair in such a manner, they would be short one presumptuous hand. But Emory looked very much like a wash-and-go girl, which I was very much not.

"Where are you from, Emory?"

"Tennessee," she replied cheerily. Well, that certainly explained the accent. "I love your dress, by the way, where did you get it?"

Ah, the dreaded "Where did you get it?" question for the fat girl. My usual go-to for when skinny girls asked me where I got my clothes was to laugh and say I couldn't remember. Because I doubted they really wanted to know or would frequent the shop anyway. There were very few conventional retailers for fat girls, some of them included the word *barn*, and I never saw a lot of skinny girls in those stores. And it's not like I could just name any popular retail store because that would be a laughable lie.

Every once in a while, I would splurge on a particularly great piece from an independent plus-size store or designer, but those were expensive, and I couldn't spend two to three hundred on just one dress. So I had to make do with the fat girl stores anyway.

I plucked at my dress.

"Um, it was actually a custom job from a friend."

Every once in a while, life threw me a bone, though.

As a fat girl with a moderately impressive following, sometimes designers asked me to wear their stuff. And sometimes those designers were my best friend from high school.

"Oh, really?" Emory sounded genuinely interested, so I went on.

"Yeah, she's A Siren Calls on Instagram and she's working on building her own brand."

"See, Emory? I told you I was dating a model!" Tobias crowed from the back seat.

I was suddenly glad it was dark outside because I could feel my face heat. And I believe it had to do with three things. One, Tobias was apparently calling me a model when he talked about me to other people. Two, he was apparently talking about me to other people. And three, he said we were dating.

"Yes, Tobias, I believed you. I just didn't believe someone as obviously cool as her would date someone like you."

She threw me a dazzling, genuine smile.

"I am cool!"

"You are so not."

Their happy, easy banter sent a pang of jealousy through me, mainly because I was still so uncomfortable. Uncomfortable in these damn shoes, uncomfortable in this burgeoning relationship. On the edge of my seat waiting for the judgement blow that hadn't come yet.

Emory reminded me of Tobias. She had an open, honest face, without guile or artifice. Maybe that's why he got along so well with this sister that was not blood.

We pulled up directly in front of the doors to Club 452 and Emory whipped out a lanyard with a VIP pass attached, which apparently included valet parking.

The valet handed her the valet ticket and she looped her arm through mine as we walked inside, Tobias left to trail behind. She had paired her band T-shirt with dark wash skinny jeans and a pair of tasseled booties.

Her gait was peppy and bouncy, and I had to hustle to keep up with my wedges.

"Dating the band has its perks." She winked at me.

"I thought you were just dating the lead guitarist?"

"Same, same."

The club was packed tight, so Catatonic Divinity must have been extremely popular, to bring so many people out to our sleepy summer town.

The air was on and large fans were positioned around the open layout, but it was still stifling nonetheless. I felt sweat pebble on my forehead almost immediately.

Emory steered us to a prime spot at the end of the bar closest to the stage. She might have been small, but she bodied her way through the crowd with ease.

Emory pulled a couple of free drink tickets out of her tight back pocket and handed them to us.

"First round's on me, cupcake."

And then she disappeared, sucked into the crowd. I assumed she went to find her boyfriend, the bestower of all our gifts.

I fanned my hot face with the tickets, arching my brows at Tobias.

"Dating the band has its perks," he repeated.

"Have they been dating long?"

He shrugged. "Couple weeks."

"Oh, nice." I was impressed that Emory was already getting VIP tickets after only a couple weeks.

His arm slid around my waist, hand grazing the curve of my ass. "Nothing is ever serious for Emory." He plucked the drink tickets out of my fingertips. "What's your poison?"

After about four fireball shots, my feet weren't hurting anymore and the band was sounding pretty damn good.

I asked Tobias what the sound actually was and he said something about indie punk rock. He also was kind enough to point out Emory's boyfriend, a lanky white guy with dark floppy hair.

I eventually spotted Emory again. She was right up next to the stage, swinging her bright mass of hair furiously.

At one point she had even bent over, hands on knees, and swung her head around wildly. The audience around her gave a wide berth, but she didn't notice or just didn't even care. She was quite literally dancing like no one was watching.

How must it feel, to be so unburdened by the opinions of other people? To move your body in any way you wanted without fear of judgement of what it was doing. To just be in the moment.

I sighed and leaned back into Tobias, whose hands skimmed my hips and belly. Catatonic Divinity wasn't really playing the kind of music for dirty dancing, but I didn't care. I wanted our bodies to fit together, every soft curve of mine filling up every hard slope and valley of his.

Tobias let out a soft gasp near my ear. His hot breath danced across my neck. I tilted my head slightly and his hot, wet mouth came down on my jugular. It was my turn to gasp at the light sting of his teeth on my skin.

I pressed myself harder into him as he kissed away the gentle ache. His fingertips dug into the soft flesh of my thighs and we swung together to the thrumming beat of the music.

"Y'all just gonna have sex right here in public?"

Emory's lilting amused voice cut through the yearning fog of desire like a knife.

I hadn't realized I had closed my eyes, so I had to open them to see her standing in front of us, face flushed, hands on her slender hips.

Tobias barely stifled a groan, his face buried in my hair.

"Emory," he growled.

"Oh, shut it. I need to pee and I need to take Bryn with me."

Emory grabbed my hand and tugged me towards the women's restroom. I was surprised by the strength in her grip, honestly. She was tougher than she looked.

We startled a couple of girls at the sink when we burst in, but they left and we were left alone in the bathroom.

Emory leaned against the sink, pressing her face close to the mirror, and was touching up her eyeliner with a pinky finger.

"I thought you had to pee?"

She fluffed up her mass of hair which was slightly damp from her exertions on the dance floor.

"Not yet."

Finished, she turned towards me and hopped up on the sink, crossing one knee over the other and staring at me with an intense and interested expression. Her shoulders wiggled.

"So, you and Tobias looked awfully cozy."

Oh, no.

I gave her a quick smile and hid in one of the stalls. I suddenly had to pee. I was accustomed to getting overly friendly with girls in bathrooms, but we were all generally very drunk. Not completely sober Emory and only slightly tipsy me. I was definitely not drunk enough for whatever conversation we were about to have.

"Is this the part where you warn me not to mess with your brother?"

She laughed. "Oh, no. Tobias is a big boy. He can take care of himself."

I flushed, straightened out my dress, and joined her at the sink to wash my hands. They were out of paper towels so I had to shake out my hands for an air-dry.

She was still giving me that intense look.

"What?"

"I like you, Bryn."

"Well, thanks. Did you have to tell me that in a public bathroom?"

"I just wanted to tell you to be careful. With Tobias. He just ended a very long relationship."

"Yeah, he told me."

"Did he tell you they were engaged?" I felt my stomach bottom out. At the look on my face, her eyebrows arched. "Guess not."

"He left that part out."

Her slim fingers danced over my arm. "Listen, Tobias is a good guy. Great, probably, even if he is mostly a big nerd. But"—she frowned at that part—"he tends to get...attached. He's not a casual guy."

I swallowed over the lump in my throat. "Did you know her? His...ex?" I couldn't bring myself to say ex-fiancée. Ugh.

"Did know? I do know. We're friends."

Oh, what tangled webs we wove. I now had a ton of questions scratching at the back of my throat, just itching to come spilling out. Emory seemed open to answering them. But I felt like that would be a betrayal of Tobias. He deserved the opportunity to explain this glaring omission. It was his relationship, no matter how close Emory was to it or how much she thought she knew.

"Do you give this warning to all his potential paramours?"

She hopped off the sink. "There haven't been any others. At least any I've heard about."

She grabbed my arm again as we walked out of the bathroom. "I didn't tell you that to scare you off or anything. Just, be gentle with him, okay?"

I squeezed her hand, glad that she couldn't read minds or anything. Because I certainly had no intentions of being gentle with him.

Especially tonight. Especially after waiting so long.

Tobias was still at the end of the bar where we left him, but his back was to me as I approached. Which I did not mind at all. He leaned on the bar with his forearms, one knee cocked. The view was intensely appealing.

There was a girl standing next to him. I didn't think much of that until her hand landed on his arm and she leaned in to laugh in his ear.

She was tall and rail-thin, all long arms and legs. She wore a tight, knee-length black and white skirt, black crop top, and strappy black heels. She had a huge mass of blonde hair that might have been thicker than her waist, which she flipped with abandon.

Game on, bitch.

I sidled on up to Tobias's other side, sliding my arm under his and around his waist.

"Hey," I said brightly and hopefully loud enough for the interloper to hear over the music.

Tobias looked down. "Hey, I thought y'all might've fallen in." His nose brushed the top of my head.

The girl's blurry eyes darted between us. She leaned in again to his ear. "You know she's fat, right?"

I'm not sure she intended for me to hear her very obvious statement, but I did, and I felt my blood run cold even in this hot-ass club.

I had spent years, years for fuck's sake, reclaiming the F word as a descriptor of my body and not a judgement of my character. People tended to wield it like a knife, nicking little pieces of me away, as if pointing out that I was fat would suddenly make me not fat. Because it worked like that.

I kept the sickly sweet smile on my face, but my hand involuntarily clenched in Tobias's shirt.

I was ready for a fight, but I needn't have worried.

Tobias affected a look of wide-eyed surprise, mouth dropping open. "Oh my God. Bryn, why didn't you tell me that? How could you keep something like this from me?"

The girl rolled her eyes, grabbed her drink, and walked off, just like that.

Without looking away, I slipped a hand under the hem of his shirt, teasing the hot and smooth skin at the small of his back.

His lips parted.

"Thank you," I said.

His large hand gripped my ass, fingertips digging into the soft and abundant flesh.

"For what," he rasped, hauling me closer, until there was nothing left between our bodies. Not even air.

In my wedges, I was at the perfect height to nip along the hard cut of his jawline, enjoying the way his beard abraded my lips.

His cock swelled against my thigh.

Hot desire flooded my body, mingled with something else...relief. He was so obviously aroused. And I did that with just my fingertips and a few rough kisses.

He wanted *me*.

I was not second to the hot skinny girl at the bar.

Who cared if he forgot to mention a fiancée. We all had secrets.

His hand fisted in my hair, pulling my head back, exposing my throat. His fierce mouth landed there, where my pulse was thumping wildly. He returned my sharp nips with teeth against the tender skin of my throat.

It was all I could do to keep my feet. My body sagged against his. I liked this sharp Tobias. He might be a good guy, a *great* guy, but a small taste of the bad guy was titillating. His fingers dug deliciously into my hips.

"Y'all really need to get a room." Emory's lilting, chiding voice interrupted...again. Tobias's warm mouth left my throat and I groaned in frustration of it all.

Emory was standing in front of us. She had given up on her hair and it was up in a gloriously messy ponytail. One hand was on her hip and her car keys dangled from the other. "I'll do you a favor."

Tobias grinned and snatched them from her hand. "You'll be okay?"

"I had planned on going home with Simon anyway. Just pick me up in the morning, okay?"

"Got it!"

"Have fun!" Emory shook her head as she walked away, amusement playing over her full mouth.

It was a little bit weird that Tobias's sister—or soon to be sister—knew exactly what kind of fun we were about to have, but I honestly couldn't care that much. As an only child, what did I know about the information shared between siblings anyway.

Keys tight in hand, Tobias leaned down, hot breath fanning over the shell of my ear. "Can I take you home?"

We didn't talk much on the drive home; we didn't have much to talk about. I didn't want to ruin the mood by saying something stupid. I focused mainly on retaining as much of my sexual confidence as humanly possible; the easy languidness of my fireball shots was a distant memory and my body was cooling, which left too much space for intrusive thoughts to come pouring in to fill the space.

Even after all this time, even after all the touching, the doubt was insidious. I was less sure of myself in the silence, when our bodies were parted.

I let out a breath.

Tobias's gaze flicked briefly to me, before returning rightly to the road. "Are you okay?" His hand slid farther up my leg, to the space where my belly met my thigh. His hand had been placed there the whole time.

I had the urge to grab it, so I did, watching as our fingers interlaced. Watching as the tendons flexed as he squeezed gently. I scratched at his hand with my nails, just barely.

"Did you like the band?"

"Honestly?"

"Honestly."

I shrugged. "They weren't too bad. Didn't focus on the music much, though." I ran my thumb over his and gave him a coy smile just in case he missed the hint.

He didn't.

The car accelerated and I couldn't decide if it was a conscious move on his part or not. I was flattered, either way.

We got back to my house safely and barely made it to the door. I had enough sense to lock it behind us, because then we were all hands and mouths and exhales, shedding clothes on our way to my bedroom. I'd have to fix that before Amera came home.

Tobias was shirtless and pantless and I had lost my shoes and mesh overdress, leaving nothing but the slinky black sheath that stuck and hugged every crevice.

He pressed up against my back, burying his face into my neck. His lips found the delicate skin of my shoulder and he placed a line of soft kisses. But I didn't want the soft boy, the good boy. That's not what his teeth promised in the club.

I took advantage of our position and ground my ass against the front of his smooth briefs and was instantly met with a groan and the pressure of a growing erection. I continued the movement, rubbing up and down along his impressive length until he exhaled, "Oh, God," and his hands clutched my thighs like a man drowning.

He held me so tight, I couldn't move. "You better stop before I get premature. I would be embarrassed." The words were breathless against my ear.

I reached up and grabbed the back of his head, pulling him in for a feisty kiss. "I wouldn't want that."

One of his hands moved up, hiking up my dress, fingertips trailing across my belly, right above the waistband of my lacy panties.

I squeezed my thighs together, body aching. I wanted him to touch me there, finally, at the hottest part of myself.

His hand slid down, down, down, fingers brushing the well-manicured mound, one finger exploring deeper, exploring every fold with agonizing slowness.

I ground down on his hand and he laughed, warm and husky.

The finger teased, around and around the general area, but not touching my swollen clit.

I moaned with despair and impatience. "Son of a bitch."

His teeth grabbed my earlobe and he made a very self-satisfied sound. "So ready."

I knew I was wet, had been hot and ready half the damn night. I could tell because his thick fingers moved with ease.

Finally, his finger moved over my clit with a slow and steady pressure that was both relief and more torture.

My legs were quivering as he stroked, calm and confident. The finger moved lower, slipping inside, and I gasped, unable to contain myself. He ground his cock against my ass to the rhythm of his finger. First one, and then two.

I'm sure I looked and sounded like a mad woman, moaning and quivering, flushed with heat. But I didn't care. Didn't care about anything other than the pressure of his fingers. They came back up, slick, and he used both to rub over my clit.

He pressed his hot cheek to mine. "Are you going to come for me, Bryn?"

His lush voice was a fan to fire.

I wanted to reply something snarky like *obviously*, or *that's a given*, but my mind was deliriously blank and the only sounds coming out of my mouth were soft huffs thanks to the deftness of his fingers.

All I could do was hold on to his shoulders as I broke apart in his arms.

Tobias held on while my breathing and pulse returned to a more normal rhythm. Not completely calm, though, because he still had his hot erection pressed deliciously tight against me.

He nipped at my earlobe. "Get naked and get on the bed."

I did not need to be told twice. We both shucked the rest of our clothes in world record time, Tobias following close behind as I climbed onto my bed. I was on my back and his mouth claimed mine in another hot kiss.

The weight of his body and the press of his warm skin against mine set my nerves on fire. His hips fit snugly between my spread thighs.

His mouth kissed a hot line down my throat, across my collarbones, down between my breasts. His cock teased dangerously close to the spot where I wanted him most.

Abruptly, he pulled back, sitting up on his heels. "Oh, fuck."

"What?"

"My condom is in my wallet. My wallet is on the floor." His fingers flexed over my thighs, as if he was loath to leave my body.

"Fuck."

"Fuck."

Well, one of us was going to have to think clearly.

I reached over for the small drawer in my nightstand, knocking over pictures and knickknacks in the process. My fingers closed over the roll of condoms and I flung them at Tobias.

They smacked him in the chest, but he managed to bring his hands up in time to catch them, an amused expression on his face.

"That works too." He ripped one off and stowed the rest in the comforter, within easy reach.

Tobias put the condom on with quick efficiency and then leaned over me with surprising speed, pinning my wrists over my head.

A breathy "Oh" was all I could manage, as the head of his cock finally, *finally* pressed inside me.

I was definitely no virgin, but Tobias was impressive, and the stretch was exquisite. He sank all the way down and then pulled back out with agonizing slowness. And then he did it again. And again.

My breathing was short and ragged and I strained against the hold he had on my wrists, wanting to touch his body. Except that Tobias worked out and I was no match for the rippling muscles in his arms, which I could see pulsate with every miniscule thrust. I strained and bucked my hips; anything to goad him into picking up the pace.

"Tobias, Jesus Christ." I moaned, biting my lip, as he sank in again.

He grinned and leaned down, brushing his nose against mine, his warm breath on my throat. "Tell me what you want."

I heaved in a breath. "Fuck me. Properly."

He pressed a kiss to my throat. And then he released my arms, his hands going to my knees and pressing my legs up and up.

I was not prepared for what "Fuck me properly" meant.

Tobias shoved inside me, so hard and deep my back arched involuntarily and I almost screamed. Almost. The sound that came out was not one I recognized.

His hands on my knees gave Tobias all the power, all the leverage, which he used to his full advantage. I just braced my hands on the headboard.

His body was a masterpiece: stomach undulating, hips rolling.

I had never orgasmed only from penetrative sex, but oh, Tobias dropped one leg and angled his body down and I felt it.

I felt the telltale pressure building in my core and I raked my nails down his back and across the unyielding skin of his round ass. My nails dug in and he bowed his head against my shoulder, breathing jagged, thrusts short and shallow.

I wrapped my arms around his neck and he came with a soft moan in my ear, shoulders shaking. I followed him over the precipice, throbbing around his cock, still buried deep inside my body.

He fell to the side with a satisfied groan. "Well."

"Well."

I stared at the ceiling, still trying to catch my breath, still reveling in the aftershocks rolling through my body.

"How was that?"

I gave him a thumbs-up. "Solid ten out of ten."

He laughed and gathered me up in his giant arms.

Tobias was right about the tiny bed. I had to be practically lying on top of him for us both to fit. Which meant a lot of sweaty skin-on-skin contact.

"I'll be right back." I pecked a kiss on his flushed cheek.

"Don't be long," he purred. There was heat still in his eyes, even though they were languid and heavy-lidded, his lips plump and smeared red with my lipstick. His eyes and lips and body promised a vigorous round two.

I climbed over him, trying not to squish any important body parts in the process, grabbed a pile of clothes, and headed to the bathroom.

After a quick cleanup, I found a pair of gray, wide-legged, lounge pants and an old T-shirt in my pile. I didn't relish the idea of just hanging out naked around Tobias with everything on display.

I unlocked my phone to find a slew of Instagram notifications and text messages. Sheenah had sent me a line of winky and kissing faces. Then there was Justin.

Hey, baby girl

wyd?

Whos the guy lol

They were spaced out throughout the night, the last one coming in about the time Tobias and I left the bar. I had posted plenty of pics of the three of us on my account. I had felt my purse vibrating, but made an effort not to check.

My heart was pounding.

While I had plenty of practice letting Justin's messages sit for a few hours to teach him a lesson, I had never just flat out ignored him before.

I tapped the message box. Typed. Deleted. Thought about Tobias, naked in my bed. Typed. Deleted.

I caught a glimpse of myself in the bathroom mirror. I looked like a hot-ass mess. Lipstick and mascara smeared. Curls sweated out. One eyelash hanging on for dear life. I did a quick cleanup of my face with a makeup wipe and brushed my hair out, pulling it up in a loose bun. I washed my hands.

I was stalling.

I looked at the messages again.

I deserved better than this, right? Three short, meaningless text messages that were only prompted because Justin had seen me with another dude. That was his modus operandi whenever it seemed like I was drifting away. Reel me back in with the right words, just the right amount of affection and longing and promises that were never kept.

It had been harder for him to do while I was away at school, but still, he managed to accomplish his mission. I might get a dick pic and a "wish you were here" any time now.

But I always let him.

It was my choice to answer. My choice to take the bait he so sweetly dangled. It was my broken heart and fucked-up love map that always answered the call.

But I didn't have to.

I could make different choices.

I stuck my phone in a basket under the sink and walked back to Tobias.

Chapter Twelve

THE WRONG SWIPE

Dear Bryn,

I am totally in love with my Civ professor and I think he might feel the same way. He always stays after class to talk to me and gives me really good grades. How do I tell if the feeling is mutual?

Hot for Teacher

NO STOP. DO NOT PASS GO. DO NOT COLLECT 200 DOLLARS.

It sounds like you're probably just a good student and he's probably just being polite. There's nothing in your letter that indicates the feeling is mutual. And, even if it is, NO. There is no universe in which trying to start something with the person in charge of your grades is a good idea.

Yes, I know, we are all technically adults, but most professors are significantly adultier than the average undergraduate. And if you still have teen in your age that man is gross and a predator. I will not be swayed on this opinion.

It's not unusual for us to get crushes on our teachers. I was in love with my freshman English professor because he smelled really nice. It happens. But the power dynamics of such a relationship make it a nonstarter. Professor and student relationships come dangerously close to breaking one of the tenets of The Wrong Swipe: consent.

You can't consent to a relationship with someone who holds significant power over you. Y'all can drag me if you want, but this isn't a movie or a taboo romance novel (DM me if you want some juicy recs). It's real life and you need to find someone else.

Hot, I'm sorry if I sound harsh—we usually like to keep it light and fun here—but I really want you to think seriously about this and make sure you are protecting your education, reputation, and heart.

Chapter Thirteen
A NARWHAL, OBVIOUSLY

Spread out over my bed, with the duvet covering only his crotch, Tobias looked like a Renaissance painting.

I thought for a second he had fallen asleep again, but his eyes popped open as soon as I shut the door.

He frowned. "You put clothes on."

I made a noncommittal shrug. I felt that laying out the full explanation for why I had put clothes on was a little much to drop on him right now.

He sat up and propped himself up nicely on a pile of pillows and patted the spot next to him. I was grateful he decided not to ask any more questions.

I crawled in next to him and made myself as comfortable as possible on his hard chest. His warm arm came down and around my shoulders.

And we were officially snuggling. After sex.

I tried not to completely ruin the moment with overthinking and just relax into the nonsexual touching.

"So, a fiancée, huh?" Yes, most excellent. Way to not ruin the moment.

Tobias let out a long and dramatic groan of the ever-suffering. "I see you have been talking to Emory."

"It's true, then?"

"Yes."

"Why didn't you mention that before?"

"Because it lasted a total of three days." His finger was idly stroking the exposed skin of my upper arm. At least, I think it was idly. It could have been a total ruse to get me off the subject. But I was not so easily distracted. "We broke up, she gave the ring back, I returned it."

"Was it a big ring?"

A snort. "No, but it was all I could afford."

"You didn't save up? Maybe that's why you got dumped."

His fingers had moved away from my arm and were creeping around to the undersides of my breast. Which was a much better ruse than my arm.

"The engagement was a last-ditch effort to save our dying relationship. I went out and bought what I could afford on a whim. So, no, I didn't save up."

"Emory seems to think it means something. That you were engaged."

"I don't really think you can count three days as 'engaged.' Besides, children of divorced parents sometimes have weird notions about relationships."

That, I could understand, as the daughter of dead parents. Well, parent, just the one.

"You don't think it's weird—"

He silenced me with a finger to my lips. "I don't really want to keep talking about other girls while I have you, right here."

His other hand had found its way to one of my nipples and was gently stroking through the fabric of my shirt. I hitched a breath. No, I didn't really want to continue talking about other girls either.

"Fair enough," I breathed, putty once again under his hands.

He positioned his body so that we were face-to-face, hand slipping beneath the waistband of my pants.

He smiled when he found no obstacles. "Didn't put everything back on, I see."

"Didn't want to make it too difficult for you."

His lips claimed mine in a slow, lingering, leisurely kiss, much different from our earlier frenzied kiss. He took his time exploring my lips, my tongue, and I did the same.

The gentleness was a little unnerving, so I nipped at his bottom lip in an attempt to bring the edge back.

It worked, but only for a few brief seconds.

Tobias was still gloriously naked, so I took the opportunity to run my palms over every inch of exposed flesh I could reach. The hard planes of his chest, covered with soft and curly hair. The hard muscles of his hips and thighs. My hands wandered lower and I was met again with his impressive erection.

I ran my nails down the velvety shaft and was rewarded with a soft moan into my neck.

"Fuck this shirt," he said.

We were on our knees on the bed facing each other and Tobias pulled the T-shirt over my head and discarded it.

His eyes immediately went to my breasts, and I resisted the urge to cover them up with my arms. Not that that would do much good.

The girls looked great in structured bras and low-cut tops, but set free they were not exactly perky. Heavy or ponderous would be more apt descriptors. I felt too exposed, too naked, without the safety net of a bra.

Tobias reached out, attempting to cup them fully for the first time, which was quite a feat. The pads of his thumbs brushed over both nipples, which hardened into tight little peaks at his touch. I sighed at the same time Tobias made a deep rumbling sound in his throat.

His hands ran up and over my shoulders, down my arms, over my breasts again, and down over my rounded belly and the silvery stretch marks there.

I wanted to run, to hide, to put the shirt back on. The mood lighting was dim in my room, but I felt like we might as well have been under a spotlight.

As his hands kept moving, my insecurities were smothered by the ache between my thighs. My want for him overruled everything else.

His fingers were dancing along the waistband of my pants. "You're so soft," he said, as his fingers dipped low. He pressed a kiss to the tip of my nose. "Lie down."

I complied immediately, lifting my hips so he could tug off the offending sweats. His hands were on my knees, sliding slowly down my inner thighs, coaxing me open for him.

I closed my eyes and bit my lip.

His hands covered every dimple and dip, the caress exceedingly slow and teasing.

My body, fed up with my dilly-dallying mind, moved of its own accord, knees falling slowly apart until I was spread open under him.

His hands finished their journey to my core, fingertips dancing over the hot and swollen flesh. His thumb found my clit and my hips bucked.

I couldn't stand it any longer. I had to see his face. So, I peeked.

His sculpted body was backlit by the rows of twinkle lights over the bed. The shadows slipped inside the hollows of his arms and chest and abdomen. The tendons in his forearms flexed with every leisurely movement of his hands. His thick and tawny hair cascaded around his shoulders like one of those heroes on the covers of the romance novels Sheenah and I had found in the school library and proceeded to check out for months when we were fourteen.

Leaning down, he pressed a hot kiss to the inside of my thigh, the long strands of his hair whispering across my taut skin.

"I feel like I'm in a romance novel," I breathed. Well, that wasn't supposed to come out.

He laughed, his breath dancing tantalizingly over my clit. "Are you a sighing damsel in need of rescuing?"

Right now, I just needed saving from his wicked mouth. From my own wants and desires.

His tongue flicked out and I gasped, stomach bottoming out at the sensation. *Fuck.*

I had forgotten why I was watching him so intently in the first place, thoroughly distracted by his body and his mouth.

I wanted to, needed to, see his face.

His head came back up, dragging the coarse hair of his beard up the sensitive inside of my thigh. I shivered.

His face, you dolt.

His face was soft and serene as he went about his work on my thigh. There was no judgement there, no hesitation, just the hint of a sly smile that portended wicked things.

The smile widened with smug satisfaction when he stuck his fingers inside me, and I moaned and arched against his hand.

I threw my head back, fully intending to go back to watching the backs of my eyelids, but his free hand came up and tangled in my hair, bringing our faces together.

"Hey," he said, "don't close your eyes."

Doing as he asked, I watched, mesmerized as his mouth nipped and licked back down my body, perfect lips finally settling on my hot core.

Then I couldn't watch anymore because I had to smother my screams with a pillow.

After, we lay tangled up in each other, legs entwined. I didn't mind it too much this time around, even though our limbs were slick and stuck together with sweat.

His fingers trailed lazily up and down my thigh.

I thought for a second he was gearing up to go for round three, but then his fingers stopped on the expanse of flesh right above my knee and I knew he had found the six, perfectly horizontal scars there.

His brow furrowed. "What's this?"

I tried for a laugh, but it was choked and raspy. "It's a narwhal, obviously."

The narwhal tattoo was something I had gifted myself freshman year and it stretched the length of my thigh to knee. It covered the scars nicely to the eye, but apparently not to the touch.

Honestly, I did not know how to respond. No guy had noticed them before. I'm not sure even Justin knew they were there. But most guys kept their hands confined to the good fat of my breasts, hips, and ass and didn't stray much further from that safe territory. No one but Tobias.

His brow furrowed deeper. "I know what a narwhal is."

"Some people don't."

"Bryn."

I flinched at the nom de plume that he wasn't aware was a nom de plume. I felt that we had reached a do-or-die moment. I either needed to open up or I would be forever holding him at arm's length. And he would know it.

I sighed.

His thumb rubbed across the scars tenderly, softly. "I'm not going to judge you."

"I had some...trouble...after my dad died." His hand stilled. "I just needed to feel something, other than the grief, you know." My hand covered his and squeezed. "They were easy to hide, here, and on my ankles." I guess he hadn't noticed those, but they were shallower and easier to mistake for the clumsy accidents of youth.

"When did he die?"

"I was twelve. Widowmaker heart attack."

That was the ironic part. My dad had been beanpole thin, didn't eat much red meat, and had no history of heart disease. That's why it's called the widowmaker. You couldn't tell that to my mom, though. My dad's death was just more ammunition in her quest to guilt me skinny. I just want you to be healthy, she'd say. I just want you to *live*.

I felt a constriction in my chest. It'd been a long time since I opened up to anyone about my dad.

Tobias pressed a kiss to the top of my head. "I'm so sorry, Bryn."

The tightness worsened and I felt the pressure of unshed tears behind my eyes.

"You don't have any pictures of him?"

I shook my head. "It's too hard."

I had pictures of him, of course, but they were stored away at the bottom of my closet in an album in a plastic box. I only pulled it out when I was ready for a good cry.

He had rescued me a week early from fat camp and then died the next day. He had been the only person to ever try to shield me from my mother. And then he was gone so suddenly and I had to learn how to shield myself.

I sucked in a deep breath and tried to regain some of my composure. What I was not going to do was have a full-blown breakdown, naked, in his arms. I didn't have enough mettle to be stripped naked, literally and emotionally.

Tobias's grip on my hand tightened, before he brought it to his mouth and kissed that too.

"Can we talk about something else now?" Before I completely lost any sense of decorum.

"Sure."

I decided to rip it off like a Band-Aid. Might as well. "My real name is not Bryn."

He froze. "Is that a joke?"

"No."

"You're not in witness protection or anything? I think I've seen this episode of *Criminal Minds*."

Funny, I'm pretty sure I knew exactly which episode he was talking about. "No, not anything like that. I sort of...remade myself when I started college."

"Okay, so now you have my full attention and curiosity." He sat up straighter on the pillows to emphasize his point.

Where to even start? "My legal name is Vivien Leigh Martin."

His mouth dropped and it was comical. "Your last name is fake too?"

"It's sort of like a pen name. I started using Bryn freshman year, and then I needed a full name for the paper, so I made one up."

"Okay, how does that even work?"

I shrugged. "It's not really hard. It's not like John Legend's real name is John Legend. Same thing. I just put Bryn as my preferred name and correct all my professors on the first day of class. Poof." I made a *poofing* gesture with my fingers to emphasize the easy.

His eyes narrowed and I could tell he was kind of shell-shocked. I didn't really think it was any different than William going by Bill or Elizabeth by Beth.

"I can't believe you gave me so much shit about being engaged for a half a second and you didn't even tell me your real name." There was a little bit of an edge to his tone that I didn't like the sound of. This conversation was going downhill, fast.

How was I supposed to explain it all to him?

"You don't understand."

"Then tell me."

I resisted the urge to huff. "Vivien Leigh is the name my mom gave me to hang all her aspirations on. Bryn is the name I chose. To escape. Because I failed her and her hopes so spectacularly."

I left out the part about me hating Vivien so much. Vivien was the quiet, fat girl who got picked on in school. Vivien got sent to fat camp. Vivien let people walk all over her. Bryn was a bad bitch who didn't take anyone's shit. Bryn was bold and cold and independent.

"How did you fail?"

It was my turn to raise my eyebrows and look incredulous. "Are you serious?"

"Uh, yes?"

"You know who Vivien Leigh was, right? The most beautiful actress of her era? Twenty-five-inch waist?"

His nose scrunched. "Never seen it."

"Oh, my God."

I think Tobias might be the first person I'd encountered who didn't know what *Gone with the Wind* was. But it was an over eighty-year-old movie, so maybe it didn't quite make a cultural impression on our generation. Or maybe it only made an impression on the kids named after the leading actress.

If Tobias had seen the movie, if he had seen Vivien Leigh as Scarlett O'Hara, he would know, without my explanation, exactly what I meant when I said I had failed my mother.

He sat up, his big hands coming to the sides of my face, pads of his thumbs skimming under my eyes. I noticed they were wet.

"Fuck everyone who's ever made you feel less than magnificent."

There was that word again. Magnificent, instead of beautiful. Magnificent hit differently. Like he was talking about more than just the way I looked, scars and all.

"Even your mom." His lips quirked in a goofy smile. "I hope that's okay to say."

I huffed out a small laugh, my hands coming up to circle his wrists. "Yeah, it's okay. I've said way worse. And to her face."

Chapter Fourteen

NEVER ASSUME EXCLUSIVITY

The lazy summer passed quickly, what with my time occupied with work, my internship app, and Tobias.

I had finally finished a few drafts of my personal statement and sent my app package to my advisor.

She and I exchanged a few drafts for edits before I had to turn in the application before the August first deadline.

To celebrate, Amera arranged for us to have a weekend at her aunt's cabin on the lake. We usually were able to negotiate a couple lake weekends, but our summer schedules gradually filled up as we got closer to finishing college.

So a combined celebratory weekend slash back to school weekend was definitely in order. I had arranged an invite for Emory, which brought our total up to five people, which made a feat of packing everyone's luggage in the back of Amera's Tahoe.

Amera put her hands on her hips, surveying the puddle of bags, water floats, and coolers.

"Sebastian, do you really need three bags for two nights? Really?"

Bastian swung around from the passenger seat and speared her with what I assumed was an outraged expression. Most of his face was obscured by a pair of outrageously huge sunglasses, so I could only guess. "Indeed."

She sighed. "Bryn only has one bag."

I surreptitiously tried to hide the overly large woven swim bag I was holding behind my back.

"She has two," Bastian returned.

"Narc," I muttered, loud enough for him to hear me. He shot me a stunning grin and returned to a front-facing position. Discussion over.

"I only have one bag," Tobias offered helpfully.

He was wearing coral shorts, a pair of casual canvas sneakers, and a cute button-down with tiny boats printed on it. He looked very lake house chic. I was wearing a cotton maxi and had only packed loungewear and swimsuits and clean underwear. I didn't plan to spend much of the weekend dressed in real clothes.

"It's a good thing," Amera muttered. "We usually put the third row down. Does Emory pack light?"

Emory was running about ten minutes late.

Tobias checked his phone. "Yeah, she's not fussy."

"I resent that!" Bastian hollered, while I said, "Are you saying that I'm fussy?"

Tobias's expression was schooled in nonchalance. "I would never say such a thing."

I bumped him gently with my hip, and his hand brushed my waist.

Amera watched the exchange and grimaced. "Gross. Well, I hope she doesn't mind being a bit squished."

She pulled half of the third row down and started rearranging the Tetris-mess that was the trunk space.

Emory pulled up a few minutes later, which was a good thing, because we only had a small spot left between the food and the booze. She bounced up to the Tahoe, peppy as ever, in a slouchy tee and frayed blue jean shorts.

She did only have one slightly oversized bag, slung over her shoulders.

"Hi, y'all!" She said with a wave.

"This is Emory, Tobias's sister."

"Almost sister," Emory peeped. "Our parents are getting married in like, three weeks."

"Amera," Amera said. She pointed at Bastian. "Sebastian, my real brother, unfortunately."

Bastian gave a small wave from the front seat, but didn't turn around.

Amera took Emory's bag and placed it gently in the free spot. She jiggled her keys. "Load up, people!"

Without a word of complaint, Emory crawled gracefully into the back seat. She looked around excitedly. "Ooh, snacks."

Tobias and I settled in the middle, my extra bag between us, and Amera hopped in the driver's seat. She turned the ignition and the shrill rip of a heavy metal guitar reverberated in the car.

"Bastian!"

He turned the volume dial down. "Sorry, sorry. I can't help it if you don't have good taste."

I couldn't see her face, but I knew her eyes were rolling. She handed him her phone. "I'm driving. I get to pick the music."

The drive to the lake house was a scenic half hour down a two-lane country road. We had just enough time for Emory to update everyone on the status of her defunct relationship with the guitarist. She hung over the back of my seat as she regaled us, myriad rows of bracelets up both arms tinkling as she gesticulated.

Tobias had a deep frown on his pretty face. I think he was taking it the hardest. The breakup would, I assume, mean no more VIP tickets for us.

Emory punched him good-naturedly in the shoulder. "Don't look so glum! Simon was such a tool."

Tobias's gaze slid to mine. "Did we just hear the same story?"

I shrugged. "I mean, eating leftovers without permission is a very serious offense."

Emory threw her hands up. "Exactly! The expert agrees with me!"

I knew Emory was probably just using the term facetiously, but I felt my cheeks heat anyway. The fact that anyone would consider me an expert on relationships and breakups was almost comical. I just happened to be a gabby goose who just happened to tap into a previously untapped and thirsty audience.

Amera must have agreed because I saw her laugh in the rearview mirror.

"Anyway, next please." Emory propped her chin in her palm and stared at the back of Bastian's head, who had missed the whole tale because he had his earbuds in.

The great thing about the Rees' aunt's house was its prime lakeshore location. It was tucked into a copse of trees at the end of a long driveway. We could drive right up to the back door and didn't have to haul any of our stuff. The expansive dock was only a short walk away and came equipped with tan-and-cream, cushioned patio furniture.

The house itself was a tidy, three-bedroom log cabin that looked how one would expect a log cabin to look. All wood interior, exposed beams, faux-worn leather furniture, plaid, plaid patterns with bears, antler lamps, and a great stone fireplace.

We never used the fireplace because we only came up in the heat of the summer and also because none of us knew how to make an actual fire.

There was air-conditioning, though, so that's all I could ask for.

The boys carried the coolers, while the girls wrangled the bags and food. Someone would have to come back out for the drinks, but I'm sure they wouldn't mind.

Amera put the several bags of nonperishables on the kitchen island as she quickly surveyed the cabin layout. There were two bedrooms and a bathroom downstairs, and the other bedroom and bathroom was upstairs in the loft.

I knew she was counting bedrooms.

Amera and Sebastian usually took turns occupying the loft bedroom, because it was basically a private suite, and therefore the prime spot in the house. But we usually only had three people. Now we were up to five.

Emory seemed to sense the dilemma. "The couch looks comfy."

Amera shook her head. "Don't be silly. You can take the pink room." So named because it was covered in pastel pink florals.

"That's only a full bed. Sebastian can sleep with me or on the couch."

I could feel a huge grin of triumph forming.

"That leaves the loft for Thing 1 and Thing 2. And get that look off your face. I better not hear any suspicious sounds."

"Wouldn't dream of it."

Once that was decided, we put away all the food and then all the bags in respective rooms and then got dressed.

I brought entirely too many suits for two nights on the lake, but I had to have options just in case I decided at the last minute I wouldn't be able to wear one of my two-pieces and needed a one-piece. And then there was the decision of a skimpier fatkini, or one with more fabric that covered more skin.

I had to keep repeating to myself that Tobias had already seen all of me, knew every curve and cleft. There were no more surprises. But there was a difference between seeing my body under the cover of soft mood lighting and seeing it bared in the sunlight.

I was here to have fun, though. This was my senior year, too. I was with my friends, with one exception. Although I didn't know her well yet, I got the distinct feeling Emory didn't give a shit about much of anything, especially not my body.

I heard Amera and Emory laughing downstairs and I knew it was now or never.

I settled on a cute black and white polka dot two-piece, with a more structured top that made the girls look fabulous. The bottoms were high-waisted with keyhole cutouts on both hips. I wrapped a mesh cover-up around my hips for an added layer of protection, grabbed my swim bag packed with sunscreen and hair ties and my phone, and headed downstairs.

Amera and Emory were packing snacks and drinks in their bags. Amera's bikini was deep red and high-waisted as well, but also high cut over her hips in a way mine was assuredly not.

Emory's string bikini was burnt orange and was leaving very little to the imagination. When she breathed or laughed, I could see the bottom of her rib cage.

Amera tossed me a towel, a White Claw, and a bottle of water. Emory loaded up a few floats over her shoulders and we headed out to the dock.

The boys were already posted up on two of the padded chaise loungers, shirtless and wearing identical oversized straw hats.

Amera and Emory dumped their things next to the other set of loungers, and then headed to the water with their floats, trailing the distinct smell of sunscreen behind them.

I stopped next to Tobias. "Nice hat."

He looked up from under the brim and grinned. "Bastian loaned it to me."

I glanced at Bastian. "Why did you bring two hats?"

Bastian was suddenly attentive, torn away from his music by Emory's sway down the dock. He tilted his sunglasses down. "Just in case one of you pasty people didn't want to get burned."

He was right on that count. As one of those pasty people, skin tone of Whitest White, I would have to be careful not to leave the lake with a nasty burn. It would be a bitch to start a new semester with a sunburn.

"Speaking of pasty"—I pulled a can of spray sunscreen out of my bag—"I need you to spray me."

Tobias jumped to attention. "It would be my pleasure."

I took my cover wrap off and stowed it away. I pulled my hair up into a messy bun to expose the back of my neck so Tobias could hit it with the spray.

I flinched when the chill spray hit my heated skin, and he quickly rubbed it in with his hand.

"Sorry."

"No worries. I'll live."

Tobias proceeded with that pattern across my shoulders, back, and backs of my things. Spray, rub, spray, rub, spray, rub. I felt like he was deriving more pleasure from the task than necessary, and I probably hadn't ever been covered so thoroughly in sunscreen. The sun wasn't getting this pasty skin today.

Not today, sun, not today.

Tobias's hand rubbed across my back and landed on my shoulder, giving me a little squeeze.

"Need me to do your front?" He'd leaned down, so his soft voice brushed across my ear.

I pulled in a shaky breath. "I think I can manage."

His fingers skimmed the soft skin of my neck, and his delicate touch promised much to come...much later.

It was going to be a long fucking day.

The boys remained on their chaises for most of the day, while I joined Amera and Emory in the cool water. I saw Tobias pull out a book. What a nerd.

Tobias was slouched in his chaise, straw hat down over his eyes and an open book on his chest.

The others had gone in for lunch, so I took Bastian's empty spot next to him.

"You're going to get a weird tan line, lying like that."

Although, I am not sure a vaguely book-shaped outline on his already tan chest would do much to mar the attractiveness of his molded pectorals.

Tobias tipped the hat back and grinned at me from under the brim. I noticed he also had a small stack of colorful, thin books between his knees. I assumed they were all poetry.

"What are you reading?"

He showed me the cover. *The Tradition*, Jericho Brown.

"Oh, a Pulitzer. Nice. Why so many?"

Tobias closed Brown's book and laid it on top of the stack. "Trying to get caught up on my contemporary canon. I have to write a thesis this year."

Tobias slouched back down, his hand coming to rest on my knee. I was impressed he was even worrying about something like that this early. The fall semester hadn't even started yet.

"What's your topic?"

He let out a much-aggrieved sigh. "That's what I'm trying to decide. I'd like to explore the rise of internet poetry and poets and their impact on the traditional poetic canon."

"You mean, instapoets?"

He shot me a look. "They've made poetry accessible and palatable to a whole generation. Is that supposed to be a bad thing?"

I held my hands up in surrender. "Okay, okay. Your area of expertise."

His hand gently stroked my thigh, almost as an afterthought. The motion raised goose bumps up and down my arms, despite the heat and high, midday sun.

"So," I continued, "what are you going to do with a poetry degree?"

I tried to keep my tone light and casual, attention turned to a pair of herons skittering over the lake. I didn't want him to feel like I was interrogating him. Honestly, he could ask the same thing about me. Journalism wasn't exactly a booming and in-demand industry to break into. There were usually more unemployed would-be journalists than decent paying, stable jobs.

Tobias rubbed a hand over his smooth beard. "You sound like my mother."

I grinned. "Sorry."

"I want to teach. College." Well, his commitment to his RA position and the high schoolers made more sense now. "I'm looking at dual MA and PhD English and Rhetoric programs for next fall."

I leaned my cleavage towards him. "Do you want me to call you doctor later?"

He leaned over the arm of his chaise, eyes gleaming, until our noses almost touched. "Don't tempt me."

I laughed. "You don't get that pleasure until you've earned it."

He exaggerated a disappointed face, throwing both hands over his heart. "You wound me!"

I laughed at him but an uneasy feeling niggled in the back of my mind. A year wasn't that long of a time, not really.

And I had been avoiding bringing up the "What are we?" conversation for fear it would send him running in the opposite direction. Against my better judgement. I had many letters in my inbox from girls who avoided that conversation and then were later hit with the "What, it's not like you're my girlfriend" lines when their erstwhile not-boyfriends did something stupid.

"Never assume exclusivity" was another The Wrong Swipe's motto. But the Bryn who wrote the advice and the Bryn who lived in the real world were sometimes different people and real life Vivien was thinking Tobias was too good to be true.

And what if I got the internship in Boston and Tobias went wherever his funded program was? What then?

Was this—were we—just a flash in the pan?

"Hey..." His warm hand cupped my chin. "You look like you're a million miles away."

A million miles away in Boston.

I nipped at his fingers. "Just thinking. About later."

"Oh?" His dazzling smile made my heart lurch uncomfortably.

Tobias leaned forward and pressed his lips to mine. It was a soft, chaste, close-lipped kiss at first that nevertheless sent my nerve ends tingling.

I wanted more.

His mouth opened, drawing me in closer, my breath quickening. I could smell him: lake water and sun and coconut bronzer. I imagined his skin would taste delicious right now.

Our quiet moment was broken by the approaching sounds of three loud voices and the thwacking of flip-flops on the deck.

I collapsed back with a huff, and Tobias with a small smile lingering on those delicious lips. He grabbed my hand, fingers entwined with mine. His skin was scorching and I greatly enjoyed the sensation.

Emory, Bastian, and Amera had come back with drinks, sandwiches, and charcuterie. I noticed Bastian was carrying most of it and was being strangely deferential towards Emory.

I raised my eyebrows at Amera and she just rolled her eyes.

Emory plopped down on the end of my chaise. "Y'all are just too dang cute."

I felt my face flush under her scrutiny. I half expected for Tobias to drop my hand. It wouldn't be the first time a guy was insulted by the insinuation that we could possibly be a couple.

Tobias's hand just flexed around mine.

Chapter Fifteen

SCREAM MY NAME

We were curled together in another tiny bed, Tobias's cock hard and hot against my backside. After all day in the sun and water, I was content to lie in his arms and let him touch me. His free hand stroked lines of fire up and down my exposed arm and leg. Every once in a while, he would stop and squeeze, as if he just couldn't help himself.

His knuckles sometimes brushed against the side of my breast, skin scorching through the flimsy fabric of my short nightgown. My nipples had gone hard as little rocks, and I could feel desire building between my thighs.

I shifted my body slightly to find some relief and Tobias made an appreciative sound in the back of his throat. He nuzzled into my neck, beard rasping along the tender flesh there and sending ripples of pleasure down my spine.

His free hand made a determined path over my thigh. I opened for him. Two fingers gently spread my folds, while a third stroked a leisurely path up and around my swollen clit.

I heaved out a great sigh.

"I want to hear you scream my name." Tobias's gruff voice danced over my heated skin. I clenched against his fingers.

Amera had said no noises in the house, but she hadn't said anything about noises *outside* the house.

I grabbed his wrist. "I have an idea."

The house was quiet as we tiptoed out, Tobias in only his boxer briefs and me in just my floral nightgown. We weren't exactly subtle if someone were to poke their heads out, especially with Tobias sporting such a giant erection.

The air was cool and moon high as we ran out onto the dock. There were also apparently motion-activated lights on the dock, which flickered to life with our presence. Those were new, but I doubted they were bright enough to wake anyone up in the house.

The sex was hot, quick, and dirty.

I knelt on the chaise, bracing my forearms on the back.

Tobias gripped my hips and buried himself inside me with a quick thrust. The chaise didn't allow much movement on my end for the spread of my legs, but that didn't deter Tobias. I gripped the cushion until my knuckles turned white as he pounded relentlessly against me.

The quick sensation was incredible; my chest heaved and my breath was coming in short gasps to match the timing of Tobias's thrusts.

I felt the climax growing and growing and then—once I was on the precipice and ready to fall—the thrusting stopped. His hips popped against mine a few more times and he let out a small groan, running his hands across the small of my back.

It was a good thing I was facedown, because that made it easy to hide my disappointment. I knew it wasn't realistic to orgasm every time we had sex; it wouldn't be the first time I was left behind with an ache in my core and a weird tingling in my chest.

But Tobias had been so different so far. I thought we were different.

I felt his weight on my back and his hot breath against my ear. "Turn over."

I froze, still stuck in my spiral of negative thoughts. "What?"

He nibbled my ear. "You heard me. Turn over."

Tobias loomed over me in the dark; he didn't give me much room to maneuver, but I did my best to wriggle over gracefully.

As soon as I was flat on my back, one of his hands curled into my hair and the other went immediately between my thighs.

I let out a very unladylike moan as he curled two fingers inside me and found *that* spot.

Our faces were close enough to kiss, but we weren't kissing. Warm breaths mingling, he took every sigh and moan from my mouth to his. Lips brushed over my cheek and jawline.

He was relentless.

I scored his back and arms with pointed acrylic nails, back arching, pressing heaving breasts against his hard chest, straps of my gown dangling off my shoulders.

I was a woman undone.

His thumb slid up and over my clit and I exploded under his magnificent hands.

"Oh, fuck, Tobias." It wasn't exactly a scream—more like a strangled, harsh whisper.

He withdrew his hand, trailing wetness across my thigh as he gripped it.

Then, he finally kissed me, deep and long.

"That's my girl."

After we had regained our breath and wits, we moved farther down the dock so I could dangle my feet in the dark water.

Tobias was wrapped around my back like a decorative cardigan, thighs bracketing mine and arms draped around my waist.

I flicked my neon green painted toes through the water. I probably wouldn't be doing this without Tobias at my back to save me if anything was lurking in the lake. Yes, I probably watched too many B horror creature flicks and I had an active imagination.

With Tobias's heavy and warm body at my back, the view was positively romantic, despite the splashes and ripples of unknown and unseen entities.

I shivered.

Tobias's arms came up and wrapped around my own. "Are you cold?"

I pressed deeper against him. "No."

"Good. Let's get in the water." He stood up suddenly and I yelped at the rush of chill air on my previously cozy back.

He quickly discarded his briefs and stood at the edge of the dock, naked, grinning at me in the moonlight. It took all my self-control not to sigh in appreciation of all his naked glory. With his tumble of hair around his shoulders, powerful biceps and thighs, and overall smooth, tanned skin, he looked like he should be the hero of a sword and sandals epic. He'd look great in a very short toga and gladiator sandals.

His teeth flashed at me in the dimness, and then he did a perfect swan dive off the dock, strapping body slipping almost silently under the water.

Oh, great. Was there anything this man couldn't do?

He popped up between my knees and I shrieked. "Jesus fuck!"

His hands ran up the backs of my calves. "Did I scare you?"

"You know damn well you did," I said, hand over my heart so it didn't shoot from my chest.

He kissed my knee. "Don't be scared. I'll protect you from anything in the water."

I highly doubted even he could save us from a preternatural swamp creature; a big fish, maybe.

I leaned forward and flicked the tip of his nose. "And who will protect me from you?"

He flashed the wolf grin and disappeared back under the water.

I stood up and shucked off my own clothes, already calculating how to best get in the water while making the least amount of noise and splash possible. I could always use the ladder, but I didn't want to look that precious.

Gritting my teeth, I took a small step and then jumped.

Tobias was right about the water. The muggy and humid summer heat had made the top layer of the lake lukewarm, but chilly down by my toes.

I surfaced to find him floating on his back, hair fanned like a mermaid.

He seemed peaceful. Heh.

We weren't that far apart, so I swam up to him with as much stealth as I could muster. If he was aware of my approach, he didn't show it. When I was close enough, I reached out under the water and poked him in the butt.

"Oh, hey now!" He rolled over rather ungracefully in the water and I chuckled.

I felt his arms around my torso before his head broke the water again. Water sluiced down his chiseled jaw, droplets gathering in his beard.

I wrapped my arms around his neck, feeling incredibly light. Our legs bumped together under the water as we both tread. The slicking of our bodies together was filling my head with dirty thoughts. Getting in the water hadn't turned out to be such a bad idea after all.

Tobias's soft lips met mine, tongue leisurely probing my mouth. I could feel his fingertips digging into the soft flesh of my bare backside. My grip around his neck tightened and we slipped under the water for a brief second.

He laughed and I sputtered, lake water in my mouth enough to cool the rising fire.

"Ack, yuck."

His arms were still on me, but I could feel him kicking harder. "I guess we shouldn't forget to float."

I swatted at his arm playfully. "It was your fault."

His torso rubbed up against mine again. "Wanna do it again?"

I pushed away from him, stretching out to float on my back, well aware of the view that would be presented to Tobias.

The growl I heard confirmed my suspicions and I smiled up at the dark sky.

I heard him splash towards me, and then his head bumped into mine as he also assumed the prone position on his back.

"Hey, I wanted to ask you something."

My stomach seized at all the possibilities that could follow that phrase.

"Yeah, sure."

"Are you free a couple Saturdays from now?"

I mentally wracked my brain for any appointments or prior obligations. I'd probably be on the schedule to work at The Bookery, but if I told Ethan in enough time, he could schedule someone else.

"Bryn?"

"Oh, yeah, sorry. I was just thinking about work."

There was a small beat of silence then, "I'm not sure if I should be insulted or not."

"No! I was just scheming how to get the time off work."

"If Ethan says no, I'll just stop by and have a little chat with him."

The image of mild-mannered Tobias confronting even milder-mannered Ethan was enough to make me snicker.

"Are you going to tell me why you might need to confront my boss?"

"Oh, yeah."

I heard him splashing around again and then his shoulder rubbed up against mine, his hand snaking through the water to grab mine. We both bobbed a bit in the water as our weight shifted.

"I'm dying of anticipation," I said dryly.

"Sorry, I think something bit me."

I squealed and flailed in the water, pushing Tobias and his hand as far away from me as possible and furiously kicking my legs to scare away anything that might be lurking beneath us.

I righted myself, the chill water sending goose bumps up my arms and legs as I submerged them again.

Once I finished panicking, I noticed Tobias was laughing as he bobbed in the water.

I cut my hand through the water, sending a spray of lake water at his head. "You ass!"

"I'm sorry, I'm sorry." His amused expression did not convey contrition at all. "I just couldn't resist."

He swam towards me, cutting through the water like a slick fish, enveloping me in his arms again, sneaky fingers tickling my sides. I tried not to flinch as his fingertips went from roll to roll.

I held on to his shoulders. "Why do I need to be free in a couple Saturdays?"

"Oh, I'd like you to be my date. To my dad's wedding."

"Won't you be in the wedding party?"

"I'm the best man, yes."

"So what do I do? Just sit around and look pretty?"

"Basically." He nipped at my ear.

"Okay, I'm in."

CHAPTER SIXTEEN

THE WRONG SWIPE

Dear Bryn,
   I think I'm in love with my boyfriend's best friend...who is a girl.
I am also a girl. Please help me!
   Might Be Bi

Oh, boy. You didn't reveal too many details in your letter, but I'm going to work off the assumption that you're not out as bisexual and may just be now discovering this for yourself.

I'm not going to pretend to be an expert on this topic, never having to have to come out myself, but this is most likely going to be a process that won't be able to be covered in one letter.

First things first, though, you need to end your relationship with your boyfriend. Y'all don't hear me side too often with the menfolk in this column, but if you think you're in love with someone else, you should do him the courtesy of breaking up. It's never nice to string someone along, regardless of sexual orientation.

Then, you're going to have to decide if or when you want to come out. How much do you know about this girl? Do you know if she has the same feelings? Do you know if she's available?

Bi, my best advice to you is to take some time to find and explore yourself as a single person, before jumping right into a new relationship. Relationships change and shape us, and you need to find out who *you* are and ultimately what *you* want.

Also, if you haven't already, I would recommend you check out The Pride Center, as they provide connection and support for our Penn Warren LGBTQ+ community. I've included their website and contact info below.

Always be true to yourselves, dear readers!

CHAPTER SEVENTEEN

PRETTY SERIOUS BUSINESS

One fresh dye job and a new set of pointy pink claws later and I felt ready for whatever Tobias's dad's wedding might bring me.

I slicked my electric green hair up into a high pony and went for big lashes—as per usual—but otherwise tame makeup. My dress was a bright yellow maxi with a sleeveless, structured bodice and a flouncy chiffon skirt. It was a good look for my body shape. A pair of cork wedges and dangly rainbow earrings completed the ensemble.

The ceremony and reception was being held at Ballard Manor, a historic, gothic villa that was an extremely popular wedding venue in our area. The manor had also, thankfully, never been a plantation. Just some dead white guy's causal country home.

It was also only about a twenty-minute drive from campus, which was a good thing for my wallet and Uber driver.

They had added a parking lot to the historic grounds, which was pretty far from the main house. I was thankful that my driver was able to squeeze up to drop me off at the top of a looped driveway that ran in front of the manor and then back down to the parking lot.

Unfortunately, I had to arrive at the venue solo because both Emory and Tobias were in the wedding party.

Tobias had offered to have me come early, but I flat out refused to just sit around and wait all damn day for the party to start. It was a nice gesture.

The manor was really beautiful, though, with its red brick façade, white columns, and blossoming white hydrangeas.

I looped the cord of my clutch around my wrist and took a deep breath, ready to enter the lion's den.

I was greeted at the door by ushers, with prizes and big smiles.

"Welcome to the Doan/Storey wedding. Sparkling water?"

I smiled and took the proffered flute, while another usher said, "Program?" and held out a program that had been turned into a fan with a little bow made of twine at the bottom. I took the fan, trying not to whack the usher with my clutch.

Hands full, I followed the crowd of people through the house and out a set of steps to the backyard.

The backyard was open to a small, half-moon courtyard covered in uneven paving stones and small white tables and chairs. Small bouquets of dark red and blue flowers sat in the middle of each table; they perfectly matched the flowers on the programs.

Through a set of double French doors, I could see a very large ballroom—like an actual, real-life ballroom—and more tables and chairs. I didn't see any food yet, which was disappointing.

The courtyard was cradled on three sides by the manor, but the fourth was open to a sloping lawn. I saw a white arch, more flowers, and more chairs at the end of a burlap aisle. It was so very farmhouse chic.

I sipped my water and liberally took advantage of my fan.

I probably wouldn't even be able to talk to Tobias until after the ceremony and whatever fancy picture-taking would need to take place after.

I was contemplating a long and arduous time by myself when a familiar form stepped gracefully into the courtyard.

"Sebastian!" I squeaked in surprise. "What the hell?"

Several heads turned in our direction at the expletive; Sebastian stepped towards me, unphased, sipping his own glass of water.

He was looking immaculate in a slim fit gray suit with a light pink tie and pocket square. He had toned down for the wedding as well, the big diamond studs in both ears the only remnant of his usual flashy style.

He clinked his glass against mine. "Cheers."

I repeated my question. "What the hell, dude. We could have hitched a ride together."

Bastian pulled a face that looked suspiciously like a grimace. "I wasn't sure if I was coming. I decided about an hour ago."

"And you just happened to have a four-piece suit ready to go?"

He rolled his eyes. "Of course I did."

Of course he did. I should know better by now. Bastian was prepared for anything. Our lake weekend was almost two weeks ago and I was surprised he hadn't said anything about it or Emory. Or that she had apparently invited him to her mom's wedding as her plus-one.

"Sooo...you and Emory, huh?"

He shrugged. "I don't really know."

I raised my eyebrows. "Family weddings are pretty serious business, you know."

"Why do you think it took me so long to decide if I was coming or not?" His dark eyes bore into me. "Do *you* know?"

Of course I knew. I had worried myself practically sick over the last two weeks planning every detail of my appearance, practicing smiling in the bathroom mirror, rehearsing lines I might say to Tobias's friends and family. Now that the day was here, I was honestly exhausted.

I sipped my water partly because of the heat and partly to calm my anxious stomach. Sebastian appeared unruffled.

Before either of us could say anything else, a petite white woman in black heels and a black cocktail dress appeared, clutching a microphone and a large planner folio.

"Family and loved ones, if I could please have your attention. The ceremony will start in approximately five minutes, so please start making your way to your seats. Thank you!"

There was a shuffle as guests started moving towards the chairs set up on the lawn.

Sebastian offered me his elbow. "Should we find seats?"

I consolidated my glass and fan into one hand and curled the other around Bastian's sinewy arm.

Relief flooded through me. Whatever his motivations and reservations, I was glad Bastian had shown up so I wouldn't have to sit through this alone.

We walked down the hill and I was doubly glad for his presence and his arm as I attempted not to step in the wrong spot and twist my ankle in my wedges.

We found some open seats in what I hoped was Tobias's side of the aisle, and Bastian adjusted ours to give us a little more space. Bless him.

There was a commotion towards the arch. I craned my head to see the petite blonde wrangling the groom and groomsmen into a tidy line.

Tobias's dad was as tall as he was, but lean where Tobias was thick. His hair was darker, silvering at the temples. He kept rubbing his palms together; a gesture born of both nerves and excitement, I would assume.

Each man was wearing a dark wash pair of jeans, tweed vest, and plaid shirts with the sleeves cuffed at the elbow. Their matching boutonnieres matched the red and blue centerpieces and the programs.

Tobias came next, followed by two other guys who must be friends or extended family members.

I saw Tobias searching the crowd before his eyes alighted on me. I'm sure I was easy to spot; I tended to stand out in a crowd. I gave a small wave and his eyes crinkled in a grin.

The officiant was shuffled into place by the harried wedding planner and then some music started to accompany the rest of the wedding party down the aisle.

There was a young boy—in a miniature tweed vest and plaid shirt—serving as ring bearer, followed by a young flower girl with bouncy blonde curls, and two bridesmaids.

Emory came next in a slinky dark red dress and a small bouquet, her long hair in a thick braid.

She smiled when she passed me and Sebastian, but it was tight-lipped and strained instead of the usual bright and bubbly.

It struck me that maybe she had ulterior motives for inviting Bastian as her date. Maybe it was less about how much she liked him—if she even did—and more as a welcome distraction during the reception. She seemed to get along well enough with Tobias, but his dad wasn't her dad. I had a feeling that maybe this day wasn't as happy for her as it was for other people.

Sebastian probably wouldn't have to dig deep into the meaning of his invite.

Once Emory had taken her place on the opposite side of the arch, Mendelssohn's classic "Wedding March" started blasting from the hidden speakers.

The crowd rose and turned to look towards the bride.

Emory's mom was the spitting image of her, except maybe an inch or two taller. Slender, with winged clavicles, she wore a loose-fitting, unadorned wedding gown that's beauty was in its simplicity. Her hair, identical red to Emory's, was cut short in a sharp bob that skimmed her cheeks. Where her dress was simple, her bouquet was ostentatious, the spray almost obscuring her face, extra flowers and ribbons dangling to the ground.

Once the bride was safely up the aisle, we sat down again, fans whirring. Sweat was beading on Sebastian's brow. I'd be glad when we could move this shindig back inside.

Thankfully, the ceremony was blissfully short.

The officiator made a small speech about love and marriage and commitment and etcetera and etcetera. Then the vows and rings were exchanged, and then the kiss.

The kiss was a sweet, chaste affair, the groom delicately handling his bride, with a hand on her cheek and on the swell of her hip.

An acoustic cover of "Don't Stop Believin'" started blaring, and apparently that was the cue. The bride held her huge bouquet in the air in triumph, and she and the groom did a strange shimmy-speed walk back down the aisle and towards the manor, the rest of the bridal party following.

The speakers squealed and the wedding planner was on the mic again. "Please join the new Mr. and Mrs. Doan in the ballroom! Dinner will be served in approximately ten minutes. Take your seats and the caterers will be around with drinks!"

I wiggled my eyebrows at Sebastian. "Drinks!"

He wiped his forehead on the back of his hand. "Finally."

I held on to his arm as we tramped back up the lawn and joined the milling of people trying to find their way into the air-conditioned ballroom.

The tables were not assigned, so Sebastian and I found an empty table towards the back, closest to an air vent, even though the sun blasting through a huge window kind of negated any air vent benefit. Sebastian slung his suit jacket over the back of his chair, loosened his tie, and rolled up his sleeves.

True to her word, waiters did start circling the room before the bridal party arrived. Unfortunately for us, they only brought water and watery "sweet" tea.

We were able to get one of each and settled in to wait on the food or the wedding party. Whichever came first.

It wasn't long before we heard the mic crackling again and the DJ announced the arrival of the newlyweds. They entered to an acoustic version of a bouncy song that sounded familiar, but that I couldn't place. Thankfully, we were not treated to any new

SOMETIMES LOVE AIN'T ENOUGH   177

husband and wife shenanigans upon their entrance—only smiles and waves.

Once they were seated, general chatter resumed with no mention of when the food was coming.

I waved my fan frantically in front of my face. Hungry and hot was not a good look for me.

"Are you okay?" Bastian asked.

"No," I clipped. "I'm fucking starving."

"Did you not eat? I always eat before these things cause you never know how long they'll take."

I gave him a sharp look. "Easy enough for you to say. I didn't eat because I didn't want to look bloated in this dress." Another tip courtesy of my mother. Fast fasting was one of her favorite activities before any kind of big event. It tended to work better when you were already skinny, though.

His lips pulled into a sharp line and I knew he was resisting saying whatever smart-ass comment had come to mind. He and Amera were well versed in my...interesting...habits and opinions about food. Usually a quick sarcastic comment made me realize how disordered I was being and then we could move on.

My mood must have been enough to keep Bastian silent.

I downed my glass of tea just to put something in my belly.

I could have fainted with relief—or hunger—when I finally saw Tobias making his way towards our table.

His hair had been pulled up and vest unbuttoned already.

"Good to see you, man." He greeted Bastian with an enthusiastic two-handed shake.

Then he looked at me and grinned, almost exasperatedly. His best man duties must've been wearing on him.

"Hey."

"I am starving."

He let out a breathless laugh. "Okay, come on." He looked at Bastian, offering his hand to me. "Emory should be around in a minute. You mind?"

Bastian waved us off.

I grabbed Tobias's hand and followed him from the ballroom.

He led us to a large kitchen area, where plates of food were being prepared for serving. Tobias ducked into the room and then returned with two buttery and warm rolls tucked in a dark blue napkin.

I almost wilted with relief. "Oh my God, I think I love you."

The words were out of my mouth before I could stop them. Heat flooded my cheeks and I quickly averted my gaze, focusing solely on the rolls so I couldn't see Tobias's reaction, or so he could react in peace. If Tobias had been just a friend, it wouldn't be a big deal at all. I told my friends I loved them all the time. But he wasn't just a friend, was he?

Stupid stupid stupid.

My hunger fugue might have just ruined everything.

I grabbed one of the rolls just to have something to do with my hands and my mouth so I couldn't make any more damning statements.

The first roll was snarfed down in no time.

Tobias offered me the second one as well. "I got them both for you."

What a dear, sweet boy.

I tore the roll in half. "We can share."

I held one half out to Tobias, but instead of just taking it like a normal person, he grabbed it with his mouth, lips and teeth skimming over my fingers.

Who knew dinner rolls could be so damn sexy?

I finally steeled myself enough to meet his eyes. They flashed with mischief.

He glanced around as if checking for onlookers, then grabbed my hand. "Come with me."

Tobias must have been spending lots of time in Ballard Manor, because he seemed to know where all the hidden rooms and alcoves were. Our next destination was a small, dimly lit sitting room.

Once inside, Tobias pressed me against the closed door, hands gripping my wrists and pulling them above my head.

I let out a gasp of surprise. "Good to see you, too."

He consolidated my wrists into one hand, the other busy with gathering up the skirt of my dress.

My breathing hitched as his knuckles skimmed my thighs.

"I've been wanting to do this since I saw you in this dress."

"Is that what you were thinking about during the, oh, ceremony?"

Tobias's fingers skimmed through my folds before finding what they were searching for, and I sagged against him, sighing. His breath was hot on my ear as he whispered, "The whole time."

He was just teasing me, those evil fingers carefully controlled. My pussy was a throbbing mess. I tried to grind down on his hand, but the hold on my wrists prevented that and sent a shiver of thrill through my stomach.

Tobias was a master at distraction. I could almost forget about my L word slipup. Almost.

I surrendered to the touch of his fingers, the press of his body against mine, the tingling of his kisses on my throat.

Chapter Eighteen

A WOMAN OF YOUR SIZE

We walked back into the ballroom holding hands and waiters had begun doling out plates of food.

Our table had grown by two random girls and Emory, who was looking as sullen as I'd ever seen her before.

Sebastian appeared to be attempting to lure her into conversation, but she sat stonily in her chair, arms and legs crossed.

As we approached, he gave me a look that quite clearly screamed, *please, God, help me*. Bastian was visibly out of his element.

Tobias took the seat next to Bastian and I greeted Emory.

"Hey, girl."

She looked up at me and I could tell she'd been crying at some point because her eyes were swollen and her mascara was slightly smudged.

I bent down so I was closer to her level and so that our words would be more private.

"Hey, are you okay?"

She gave me a long, measured look and I knew she was deciding whether or not to trust me with whatever she was dealing with.

Her mouth tightened and I knew she had decided against it. "I'm fine." She physically let down the tension in her shoulders. "Let's eat."

"If you need anything, we can talk."

She gave a sharp nod, and I knew I wasn't getting anything else out of her. At least, not here and now. I felt sorry for Bastian. It seemed like he'd be a loner at this wedding after all. Emory did not look like she was in the mood to party.

I took my seat next to Tobias and nudged him in the ribs, gesturing to Emory with my chin.

He didn't look at her, but pulled his phone out of his pocket. A second later, I felt mine buzz in my clutch. Oh, this was going to look real subtle.

I gave it a few seconds, but realized no one was paying us any attention. I checked my phone quickly.

Tell you later. Divorced parent stuff

Well, that would explain it. Maybe Emory wasn't as keen on getting a stepdad as she appeared to be on getting a stepbrother.

A few waiters arrived with our plates, and refills of water and tea. Emory snagged one guy before he could leave. "Four shots of vodka, please. Top shelf." He grinned at her and left.

Well, shit. Maybe Emory was partying tonight after all.

After three top-shelf vodka shots—which, by the way, didn't taste any better than cheap vodka—Emory was back to her old self. Bubbly and bright Emory had returned, fueled by the alcohol.

That was one way to resolve her feelings over the wedding.

We were all feeling the effects of the alcohol...just in time for the dancing to start. The DJ started playing "I Wanna Dance with Somebody," which flooded the dance floor with people, Emory and Bastian included.

Tobias's cheeks were flushed and his hair delightfully mussed. I leaned in close and ran my fingers through it. The spicy tang of his cologne tickled my nose. He leaned into my touch like a cat.

The vodka shots had put a big, goofy, lopsided grin on his face. He traced my jawline with his finger, then ran down my throat, and played with the strap of my dress, perilously close to the soft, pale skin at the top of my breasts. I felt my body heat with pleasure and the slight thrill of people seeing his brazen touch.

His roaming fingers brushed the top of my dress before settling on my hand. "Come on. There're some people I want you to meet."

Oh, great. He decided to do the introductions *after* I'm already three vodka shots deep. This was either going to go very well, or very terrible. I wanted to be nervous, but the vodka was handling that. I knew, being invited to a family wedding, that I would most likely be meeting the parents.

Tobias tugged me along, navigating in and out of the gyrating bodies on the open dance floor.

We ran into his dad and Emory's mom first, Stan and Margot. Stan stood every inch as tall as Tobias and had a thick head of salt-and-pepper hair. He shook my hand very enthusiastically when we were introduced. Both he and Margot bore wide smiles and looked extremely happy.

As Tobias tugged me away, I saw Stan kiss the back of Margot's hand with reverence.

It made me happy to see them both get their second chance at love.

I was feeling all mushy and gushy inside when we ran into a statuesque woman who had Tobias's eyes. My stomach sank. The Mother.

Tobias's mom was a tall, blonde, shapely woman in a tight red dress. She was clearly styled in a way that screamed, *Look at what you're missing*.

I was momentarily stunned. Was it normal wedding etiquette to invite the ex-wife to the wedding for your new wife? Was this why Emory was so upset? Were they all playing the parts of happy blended families, and this was just part of the charade?

She smiled at me, but her eyes were flinty whereas Tobias's were always so soft.

"Mom!" he chirped.

"Toby, my love!" she said fondly. They embraced, and she kissed his forehead softly. It was all so lovey and maternal, that I was chiding myself for judging her so harshly just seconds ago.

"Have you seen your father? I haven't had the chance to congratulate the newlyweds yet." There was a sharp edge to her tone that had me reevaluating her again.

"Yeah, we just saw him. Over there." He gestured vaguely in the direction we'd just come from. "But I wanted you to meet someone." His arm slid around my waist and finally her attention landed fully on me. It was not a pleasant feeling to be under her gaze. Even in my wedges, she was taller than me, and had to look down her slim nose at me.

Her smile was wide, but cold. "Of course, love."

Tobias apparently didn't notice anything amiss. "Mom, this is Bryn. Bryn, this is my mom, Sandra."

"Pleased to meet you, Mrs. Doan."

"Not anymore," she said curtly.

I tried not to wince.

"Mom, really."

She sighed theatrically. "Sorry, dear. I didn't mean to drag you into our messy family drama."

She simpered for Tobias's benefit, but her apology was about as fake as her hair extensions. She knew what she was doing.

Something or someone had caught Tobias's attention. He waved off into the crowd. He squeezed my hip, said, "I'll be right back," and then evaporated as fast as my liquid courage.

I was left alone with Sandra, Alpha Mean Girl. *Fuck.*

I managed a smile. "It was a pleasure—"

She cut me off when she suddenly gripped my shoulders, like we were old friends and she was happy to see me. Her hands were cold.

"Oh, honey, you look really beautiful for a woman of your size."

And then she was gone as fast as Tobias, leaving me gaping and alone in the middle of the dance floor.

Suddenly it was too hot in the ballroom, despite the air-conditioning. My skin was too tight. I couldn't breathe. I needed air.

I muddled my way back through the manor, until I was able to escape onto the front porch. The sun had finally set, so it wasn't so oppressively hot. There were a few secluded wooden benches at the corner before the porch turned around towards the back of the manor where I took refuge.

My chest was tight. I could feel the pressure behind my eyes of unshed tears. I wanted to just break down and cry so badly.

It wasn't even what Sandra said. The "your size" barb was familiar and common and not really even that creative. *You're so pretty for your size.* It wasn't her words that stung. It was her tone, the curl of her lip as she walked away. Her insinuation that I was trying too hard and still failing. And I was trying hard. Every day I woke up and it was a battle to prove that I was more than my body and what people thought of it. Every day was a battle to be pretty, to be put together, to be productive, to prove I was worthy of love and respect. That I was worthy of Tobias.

And Sandra so clearly thought I wasn't.

That's what stung. And I was so damn tired. Tired of all the waxing and shaving and plucking and trying not to breathe too hard or step too heavy. I just wanted to burn it all down.

To get a break from the swirling molasses of my thoughts, I pulled out my phone to do some mindless browsing.

I had a few new unread texts.

From Sheenah: *YOU LOOK GORGE. Have fun with your man mammoth*

And then from Justin.

Long time no talk haha

I sighed. It was just the latest in a one-sided string of texts that had gone unanswered. But it was dark and I was hurt and my resolve was weakening. It was literally the longest I'd ever gone before ignoring him.

My thumbs hovered over the keyboard.

"Are you out here hiding?"

Bastian.

I clicked my phone off.

He sat down next to me on the bench, leaned back against the brick, and crossed his legs.

"I'm not hiding."

"Are you sure?"

"Tobias's mom called me fat."

His eyes widened. My straight-sized friends were always shocked when they heard about the casual nastiness otherwise normal, regular people leveled my way. Oh my God, the amount of people who thought they had a right to comment on the bodies of fat people. They still thought it was okay. Just couldn't keep their fatphobia to themselves.

"What a bitch," he said.

"I would agree." I slouched against the back of the bench, thumb fiddling with the squishy glitter case on my phone.

"He's never going to choose you, you know."

His voice was soft, but I was startled nevertheless. "Who?"

Bastian nodded to the phone in my fidgety hands. "You know who. The guy you're about to text when you know you shouldn't."

I made a conscious effort to still my hands. "I am not." He snorted. "Okay, yes I am. How did you know?"

"You have that look about you. Sad and lonely."

I wanted to feel insulted, but Bastian's tone was almost wistful, not judgemental. He leaned his head back against the brick.

I raised an eyebrow. "How many more shots did you have?"

He grinned. "Enough to try to save this party."

I leaned against him, resting my cheek on his shoulder. "Going that well, huh?"

He patted my knee. "Just about as well as yours."

"Oh, good. So it's an absolute trash fire."

I was toying with my phone, toying with the idea of finally texting Justin back, when I felt it buzz in my hand. For a brief moment I thought it was Justin again, but the preview that flashed up on the screen said it was an email from Dr. Mal Leeland. The director of the Boston internship.

I almost dropped the phone in my haste to unlock the screen. "Holy shit."

"What. Did you text him?" Bastian peeked over my shoulder.

But I was shaking my head emphatically, hands practically trembling as I opened the email.

Dear Ms. Martin,

Congratulations!

You have been selected as one of the finalists for our annual summer internship program. The committee and I will be holding interviews at Western Kentucky University August 30th through September 3rd.

Your scheduled interview time is 9:00 a.m. on September 1st. Please come prepared to discuss your work, application materials, and your goals for the program.

If you have any conflicts with this time, please notify the committee immediately via the contact information below.

Yours cordially,

Dr. Mal Leeland, Director

School of Communications

I squeaked and Bastian shook my shoulders. "Girl, you did it!"

"Hardly. It's just an interview." My pulse was racing and my heart skittered around in my chest. An interview. I didn't have any conflicts because I didn't have any classes on Wednesdays. WKU was about two hours away, so I'd have to find a way to get there, but that was the easy part.

"That's basically halfway there. And you'll kill an interview."

Bastian's vote of confidence was bolstering. I *could* kill an interview. I could be bubbly and jovial and enthuse about my work and get near-strangers to like me. Well, maybe not if they were anything like Sandra, but I'd cross my fingers and hope for the best.

Bastian and I decided to Uber home together not long after our front porch heart-to-heart. We ghosted our respective dates, and I tried not to be salty about the fact that Tobias didn't appear to notice.

After I got dropped off, I immediately discarded my wedding attire on my bed, pulled on my coziest pajamas, put on a hydrating face mask, grabbed a glass of milk, and settled down on the couch to watch an episode or two of *Criminal Minds* and relax. Odafin found his way into my lap for ear scritches.

Not thirty minutes into my first episode, the doorbell rang, sending Odafin skittering for cover. I frowned at my phone, dark and silent on the coffee table. Who, in the year of our Lord 2021, shows up at someone's house and rings the bell without a heads-up?

I reluctantly got up from my cozy spot and peeped through the small glass window on the door.

Tobias leaned against the doorframe, looking equal parts disheveled and sexy, his vest gaping open and his hair a mad wave around his face and shoulders.

I took a deep breath before opening the door.

He was standing there, grinning. "Nice face mask."

"Oh, shit."

His amused laughter followed me as I scurried to the bathroom to peel off my face mask and wipe away the excess gunk with warm water and a towel.

When I came back out to the living room, Tobias had taken off his shoes and vest and was in my spot on the couch.

I double-checked that the front door was locked before joining him.

"I'm glad you came over," I said.

He grabbed my hand and turned it over so he could kiss the back of my wrist. "Why did you leave without saying anything? I would have come with you."

I shrugged and tried to sound casual. "I didn't want to interrupt your night."

"It wasn't as much fun without you there. We didn't even get to dirty dance to early aughts rap songs."

I snorted. I'm sure his mother would have greatly appreciated that show.

He ran his fingers over my forehead and through my hair. "Are you okay? Like, for real?"

I cupped his face in my hands. "Just hot and tired."

After that we got more comfortable on the couch. I reclined against one of the plush arms and he laid between my legs, arms around my waist and face snuggled into my chest. I propped one leg on his butt and played with the loose strands of his hair.

The TV droned in the background as I opened with, "So, um."

His head popped right up, jerking the fingers I had tangled in his hair. "What?"

"I got an interview. For the internship."

His face broke out into a wide, slightly lopsided, slightly drunk grin. "You are brilliant. Brilliant and magnificent." And then he snuggled back down into my bosom.

His solid weight on top of me was easy and comfortable. It wasn't long before his weight got heavier and I heard the light snuffles of a quiet snore. Odafin creeped back into the room and decided the ideal spot for him to lay was in the small of Tobias's back, making biscuits in his ass.

I stroked both boys' heads and smiled.

If this felt so good, then why did I still feel so bad?

Chapter Nineteen

WHAT KIND OF WEIRDO

The week before my interview it was all hands on deck.

Sheenah kept texting me motivational and inspiring memes she found online.

Amera and Bastian helped me prep and practice possible interview questions. Amera was actually helpful; Bastian less so. Since I really didn't expect the interview committee to ask me if I were a top or a bottom.

Tobias was a tall, steady bulwark of support. The calm in the storm.

When I finally had my requisite breakdown three days before my interview, he held me, stroked my hair, and kept repeating how brilliant I was.

The Tuesday before my interview, Tobias was supposed to meet me in the dining hall between classes.

Since I moved off campus, I didn't have cause to use the dining hall very frequently, but it was a bright, airy space that was conveniently located to meet friends for lunch.

Tobias had texted that he was running a couple minutes late, so I grabbed a coffee and busied myself in some work, letting the soft crash of voices drown out negative thoughts.

I was deep in my Moleskine journal, drafting possible answers to the inevitable, "So why should we choose you?" question. Writing my thoughts down helped me remember any clever turn of phrase I happened to come up with.

He slid into the booth and thunked something hard onto the top of the table.

I put my pen down and gave the item my full attention.

It was a plant.

"It's a plant," I said.

"*Crassula ovata,*" he said.

"Come again?"

The little plant was in a white pot, with white stones around the base. It looked a little bit like a tiny tree, with shiny, round, thick leaves.

"It's a jade plant. They are supposed to bring good luck. It's for you." He scooted the plant a little closer to me while I tried not to just burst into tears.

"I'm going to kill it," I said, my voice strained.

"No, you won't. They're hardy. Just remember to give it enough sun and not too much water." His directions were so simple, and yet I had so little confidence in my ability to keep the jade plant alive.

I turned the pot around in my hands, my nails clicking around the ceramic. "Are you sure?"

"You can do it, Bryn."

Then he reached across the table and twined his fingers with mine, here, in such a public place, in front of so many onlookers. I'm sure Tobias's presence didn't go unmarked when he was around on campus. My stomach churned with nerves.

"What if I can't?" The confession was whispered, and I wasn't sure he'd even heard me, except for his response.

"You can. Just be yourself."

"Right."

And who was she?

Emory, bless her heart, agreed to drive me to the interview, although the morning of, it looked like she regretted that bit of magnanimity.

She pulled up in men's basketball shorts, a band shirt, and large sunglasses, nursing an enormous cup of coffee.

She held up another cup as I climbed into the car—after buckling Rossi the jade plant into the back seat. "White chocolate mocha. Tobias said that was your favorite."

I nodded and took a grateful sip. Between doing my hair and doing my makeup, I'd barely had enough time to gulp down a protein bar, much less brew my own coffee. Amera had helped me decide on an outfit the night before, or I would have really been struggling.

It honestly wasn't that hard of a decision because I did not have that much that would be considered business casual and interview appropriate. I had interviewed for my job at The Bookery in leggings. I had a feeling the interview committee wouldn't be impressed by that.

I smoothed down the front of my dress, which was a blue and black herringbone with short sleeves and an appropriate neckline and hemline. Small pearl studs and sensible black wedge heels completed the look.

Emory glanced over at me, one hand on the wheel and one on her coffee. "You look...subdued."

I tugged again on my hem self-consciously. "Yeah, well. Can't have too much cleavage running about at these sorts of things."

She chuckled, gaze going to the rearview mirror. "I can't believe you brought the damn plant."

"Tobias said it would bring good luck." By my logic, it wouldn't do to have my good luck stuck in my room. It probably worked better if I kept the luck close by.

Emory executed a particularly risky move entering the highway and I had to grab the oh-shit handle, glancing back to make sure Rossi hadn't fallen over.

We were definitely not going to be late because of her driving. Dead, maybe, but not late.

"So, you and Tobias. Plant coparenting, huh."

I felt my face flush. But why was I flushing? "No. Well, I think he expects me to keep it alive by myself." I was doing a pretty good job so far, but it had literally been less than twenty-four hours. "Will he be upset if I kill it?"

She snorted. "He may be vaguely insulted, but I'm sure he'll recover." She accelerated and I closed my eyes. "So, what did you think of the wedding?"

Emory's voice was trying so hard to be casual, but there was an edge there. I hadn't talked to anyone about the wedding since it ended. I had been too preoccupied with my interview, and I had the feeling that it had been rather uneventful for everyone else except Emory and me.

I tried looking at her without looking at her, but I didn't have any sunglasses to hide my gaze. Was she finally going to tell me what she thought of the wedding?

"It was really pretty." That was true. "Oh, I met your mom! She was beautiful." Also true.

"Did you meet Tobias's mom?"

I clasped my hands together to stop their fidgeting. I didn't owe anything to Sandra Doan, that was for damn sure. But I didn't want it to get back to Tobias that I thought his mom was a raging bitch. We didn't have enough history for *that* kind of honesty.

"Um, she was...fine."

Emory barked out a laugh. "You can be honest, you know. She called my mom a gold-digging whore when they got engaged. And Stan doesn't even have that kind of money."

"Oh, well, then. Yes, I met her. And yes, she was a total bitch."

"What'd she think of you? She thinks I'm a pot-smoking underachiever."

I didn't really want to tell Emory what Tobias's mom thought of me. It still felt too fresh, too raw. I didn't want to plant that seed in her brain too: that I just wasn't good enough.

So I just said, "Fat."

Emory snorted again. "Don't let perfect Miss Sandra get to you. She hates everyone except Tobias."

I finally had the nerve and the opening to ask what I was really dying to know. "Why the hell was she invited to the wedding?"

"She wasn't. But no one had the balls to tell her that."

Oh, Jesus. Sandra was one gigantic piece of work. "I'm beginning to rethink my attraction to your brother."

Emory let out a peel of laughter that was a refreshing return to normal. "You probably should. I mean, what kind of weirdo gives a girl a plant?"

Emory dropped me off in front of the communications building, where the interviews were being held, and zoomed off with Rossi still in the back seat. I had briefly considered taking him with me, but didn't think that would go over well with the committee. My stomach was a hot ball of nerves.

It was just another Wednesday for everyone else milling about and no one paid me much mind as I wandered the building, consulting the extremely vague directions on my phone.

By the time I found the correct room, there was only ten minutes to spare before my scheduled time. Bless Rossi and bless Emory and her temerarious driving.

There was no one else in the hallway, so I sat on the bench to wait.

I was idly scrolling my phone to pass the time when Shaw black heart emoji popped up on the screen. Once, twice, and then a third time.

I chewed on the side of my lip. He had literally the worst timing. I considered not looking at the texts at all and leave them sitting in my phone to deal with later. But curiosity got the better of me.

I don't know what I did, but I'm really going through some shit here Vivi you are supposed to be different than the rest of them

You're my best friend

I thought I could count on you

Tiny words on a screen, but they cut through me like a physical force. It was the most I had ever seen Justin write in a text, so there must be something really serious going on. The apology was right there, hovering on the tips of my fingers. He had never been mad at me. I had never *let* him get mad at me.

You are supposed to be different.

I had made a point of being different from the rest of them. So different, so that I would be able to stand out in ever-revolving door of girls in and out of his life. A very Not Like Other Girls girl.

I was briefly aware of someone saying my name, but I was still staring at my screen, messaging app open and waiting, guilt and dread curling around the nerves in my belly.

"Ms. Martin." The woman's voice was slightly louder than normal now. My head snapped up. "Are you ready?"

The woman standing in front of me was young and slim, wearing a pencil skirt and heels, with a folio propped on one arm. Her winged eyeliner was impeccable.

She gave me a small, polite smile when we finally made eye contact.

"Um, yes, sorry." I fumbled with my phone and purse, stuffing the offending device deep in its bowels.

I stood up and took a small breath, but it was hardly enough to still my shaking hands.

Justin had hurt my feelings before, on multiple occasions. That was nothing new. But it also never felt deliberate. This felt different. This felt like he had sat there and chosen the words he knew would cut me the most.

The woman gave my shoulder a small pat as she gestured me into the room. "Don't be nervous."

It was already far too late for that.

The room was unbearably cold and clinical.

I was usually a big fan of air-conditioning, but goose bumps broke out up and down my arms and legs as I sat down in the horribly uncomfortable chair that was obviously there for me. Were they trying to make applicants miserable?

I tried to make myself as comfortable as possible, smoothing the front of my dress and attempting not to squirm too much.

The lone chair was stationed in front of a long gray table, my four interviewers occupying enviously cushioned chairs behind it, facing me.

There were two older white men and two women, one of which was pleasantly on the plump side. I took another moment to breathe and take heart in that, as it was a good sign that fat women were welcome in this space. They were all dressed appropriately college professor-y in blazers and earth tones.

The woman who retrieved me from the hallway must have been the department secretary or admin, because she started handing out a stack of papers to each of them. I assumed it was my application packet.

She said, "Vivien Martin" and then it was time to begin.

They asked me softball questions for the first five or ten minutes; stuff that was easily figured out by my application materials. Honestly, I appreciated the soft opening, so I had more time to collect my thoughts and push Justin to the back of my mind to be dealt with later.

Things were going well until one of the men asked me to expand on the significance of my work and I took a moment too long to think and felt my purse buzz against my ankle.

It was enough to cause my heart to stutter and I looked down, only to feel the buzz again and wonder what Justin was accusing me of now.

"Ms. Martin. Do we not have your full attention?" It was the plump woman and her sharp voice.

I looked back up only to see her make a quick mark on the paper in front of her.

Oh, fuck.

"No, Dr. Hall, um, I mean, of course." I felt the heat drain from my face and my hands went cold. I clasped them together tightly, fingers grinding together. "I was just thinking, um, my work is all about the sexual empowerment and agency of women."

More nodding and scratching of pens, but I felt the damage had already been done.

The phone continued to buzz against my ankle.

Emory was idling in the faculty parking lot outside the building, a loud, unfamiliar band blasting from her open windows. Several groups of passing students shot her dirty looks and she gave them the finger and a smirk.

I stumbled down the stairs, practically in tears, but hitched on a smile as I climbed in the passenger seat.

"It went that well, huh?" she asked, peeling out of the parking lot.

"Sure did." I could hear the tremor in my voice and I'm sure she could too. I bundled my purse on my lap, finally pulling out my phone.

It wasn't even Justin. It was my mom calling and texting. I had mentioned the interview to her, so I'm sure she was calling to check on me. I read her texts.

Make sure you don't wear too much makeup.

It's not Instagram.

Yeah, thanks, Mom.

"Do you want to talk about it?"

"Not really."

I wanted to put the interview as far behind me as possible. I knew I had fucked it up. They would remember me as the distracted girl, and even if they otherwise liked what I said, that would be a mark against me.

And I didn't really feel like explaining to Emory *why* I was so distracted. It would hurt too much, to admit that I'd let my guard slip again and Justin slithered back in. And I had let him.

I pecked back a quick response to Justin, barely looking at the screen, the letters on the keypad more muscle memory than anything.

Sorry.

When we got back to the house, Tobias, Amera, and Bastian were all squeezed on the living room couch.

They cheered enthusiastically when we entered, but out of the corner of my eye, I saw Emory slice her hand across her throat in the universal "Oh, shit, stop talking" gesture.

I cradled Rossi in my arms and went straight to my room. I discarded my shoes in the middle of the floor and put Rossi on the spot I had made for him on the windowsill, nestled in the gauzy pink curtains.

"Hey."

Tobias was leaning against the doorjamb. And, hot damn, the boy could lean. He took up almost all the space in the doorway with his mile-long arms and legs. He looked especially delicious today in his tight jeans and shiny, cognac boots.

"Hey." I pressed the heels of my hands against my eyes, heedless of my mascara and eyeliner, willing my body not to betray me this way by sobbing uncontrollably.

"Emory said you were upset."

I shook my head, not trusting myself to speak. I still couldn't look at him because I knew what I would see. Those big, luminous, stormy blue eyes that would no doubt be filled with genuine concern and empathy—feelings I didn't deserve. I felt my throat constrict, and a small, pitiful sound rattled in my chest.

"Hey there."

I didn't see him move, but I felt the warmth of his body fill the space in front of me and then his palms were on my shoulders. I couldn't help it. I sunk into his embrace, pressing my face to his sternum, inhaling the musky cologne that lingered in my bed even when he left. My hands clutched his shirt. I may not deserve him, but I wanted him; I wanted to deserve him.

His hands rubbed my back in soothing circles. "Interviews are hard. I'm sure you did fine. If you want to talk about it, I'm here, okay?"

I nodded into his chest. Miraculously, the tears never came. His touch was anchoring; I felt like I was coming back to my body. The interview almost felt like a distant memory. Justin wasn't, though. He felt like a fresh bruise.

I finally pulled back. "I just need a little space to process. Ruminate on my failings, you know." I smiled like it was a joke.

Tobias cupped my face and pressed a kiss to my forehead. "Sure. I'll clear out the spectators." He trailed his fingers down my arm and tangled them through mine and left my room like there was nothing amiss.

Except he didn't know about Justin and he didn't know how weak I was and he didn't know my loyalty had always belonged to the dark-eyed boy who'd carved his name into my heart when I was only fifteen.

And I didn't know how to wash him off me. Didn't know if I could break the cycle. Didn't know if I was strong enough.

CHAPTER TWENTY

THE WRONG SWIPE

Dear Bryn,

I'm currently in a relationship that's lasted several years. It's my longest relationship to date. But here's the issue. I can't stop thinking (sexually) about and flirting with other people. I've never fully cheated (is that a thing?) but I've definitely come close and I've definitely strayed emotionally. I love my partner, so why am I like this?

Wandering Eye

Hi, Wandering! I think you are asking the wrong questions. It sounds like you are putting a lot of pressure on yourself to sustain and maintain long-term relationships and I would ask you...why?

You're young! You're in college! I know monogamy is socially engrained in us as a society and, especially for women, achieving the ultimate gesture of monogamy (marriage) is considered a high and desirable achievement. Solve world hunger? Meh. Get married? SUCCESS.

I have a lot of feelings on this topic, but I want to say this: only 3–5% of mammal species practice any sort of monogamy*.

You say you love your partner, but what about yourself? It sounds like you're in a relationship dynamic that is making you unhappy, so something is going to have to change. I still think you should treat your partner with respect and dignity, even while doing what's best for you.

So, Wandering, you need to talk to them. And it needs to be face-to-face. No email or text Feelings Bombs. There could be other options here, other than breaking up. Maybe your partner would be amenable to an open relationship, maybe you two could explore polyamory. But the most important part is that the communication needs to occur and if you're changing the dynamic of your relationship, your partner needs and deserves to know.

It's probably going to be hard, and there might be some hurt feelings, but you deserve to be in a relationship (or no relationship) that's meeting your needs.

*I Googled it

Chapter Twenty-One

GREEN HAIRED GIRL

The next night, Tobias invited us to a poetry reading at Penny's Place, which was on the bottom level of one of the other dorms and was connected to the dining hall by a concrete walkway and a courtyard that was a popular gathering spot for students.

I could only convince Amera to come with me.

Emory had a night class and Sebastian flat-out refused to go to a campus event on Thirsty Thursday.

The café was actually quite large. The display case and registers were separated from the seating area by a long bar lined with backless barstools. The regular seating area was a mix of short tables, high-top tables, squishy chairs, and tan couches. Everything was angled slightly towards an oval-shaped, raised stage in the back corner. Student art and campus promotional posters littered the walls.

It was a cozy, quintessential collegiate joint.

"We have open mic night every Thursday," Tobias said excitedly. I got the distinct impression he spent a lot of time here. "You all find a seat. I have to go talk to the emcee." And then he was off.

Amera raised her eyebrows. "He is such a nerd."

I nodded. "Have you ever been to one of these things?"

"Are you kidding me?"

I would take that as a no, then.

We surveyed the room for seats. High tables and the bar were out, because I was not forcing my body to endure the pain of that for however long we were here.

"You pick seats, and I'll get drinks," Amera said, walking off towards the register.

I gave her a thumbs-up right as I spied two open plushy chairs next to the windows. I hurried over to grab them, swinging my purse into the other empty chair to protect it for Amera.

Turns out I didn't have to fight anyone, and she arrived soon with two very large, very pink, very refreshing drinks.

She pulled two metal straws out of her bag and handed me one. "Here, save a turtle."

I poked the straw in her direction. "You're the real MVP."

I had a collection of metal straws that kept getting bigger because I would forget them in drinks or forget to wash them and then they'd grow...stuff. And then I'd have to replace them and then I would forget to bring them with me when I'd go somewhere that required a straw. Sorry, turtles.

Amera and I sipped our drinks, and I observed the student body around us, most of which were female. That was interesting.

I figured out why when Tobias loped gracefully onto the small stage. The girl directly in front of me let out a small sigh.

Tobias had to extensively adjust the microphone to fit his abnormal height. He smiled and said, "Tall people problems," and the gathered crowd laughed. He acted like such a natural under the stage lights. He looked like some kind of golden-haired Viking god descended from the sky to bless us all with his presence. He wore a long, fitted green T-shirt over his usual jeans; hair a riot of waves around his shoulders. He also had on some corded bracelets and a necklace that looked suspiciously inspired by Emory.

Once he had the mic settled, he pulled a neatly folded stack of paper from his pocket, which he unfolded with a flourish.

"I have some new stuff for you all tonight." There was cheering and the sighing girl in front of me almost swooned.

Amera gave me a panicked look. "Oh, God, he's reading poetry?"

I snorted into my straw.

Tobias's poetry was actually really good. The first one was a light and humorous sonnet and the second was a highly structured villanelle where he was clearly flexing.

Tobias took a quick break to sip from a bottle of water, and I took the opportunity for a quick social media break.

That's when Justin called.

I hit the power button before Amera could see. But he called again...and again.

Tobias was still on break, chatting with the emcee and a few of his enthusiastic fans. If I were quick enough I could I slip out, find out what Justin wanted, slip back in, and finally move on from whatever crisis Justin was having that apparently required my attention.

I put my drink down and whispered, "I need a minute."

Amera's eyes narrowed.

I left the café and went to hide behind a pillar and called him back. He answered immediately.

"Vivien, thank God."

"What do you want?"

"Can you not be that way?"

I chewed on my thumbnail. Be what way? Wanting to know what he wants because he always wants something?

"I'm going through some shit here, baby girl."

I tried not to sigh too audibly. He was always going through something or other. He probably just wanted an emotional boost to his ego and then we could go our separate ways for months again. I could do that. I softened my tone. "What's going on, Justin?"

He made some inaudible noises on the other end. "It's Bekah. She says she's pregnant. But I don't think it's mine."

All the air left my lungs in a whoosh. "Justin. You got a girl pregnant?"

"I don't know."

The hand holding my phone started shaking and I felt my heart thudding dully in my chest. What was this feeling? Panic? Despair? Was he supposed to choose me over his pregnant girlfriend?

"Vivien." His voice cracked. "Tell me what to do."

"I don't know. Justin, what do you mean you don't know if it's yours?"

"There's another guy."

"Are you going to get a paternity test?" That was the most logical thing to do. Something like relief flooded my chest. And wasn't that awful.

"Do you think I should?"

"Justin. Of course. If you're not married, there's no assumption of paternity. You want to get a paternity test."

"Right." He sighed. "That makes sense. I knew you would know what to do. Are you coming home soon? I really want to see you."

"I'm not sure. I'll let you know if I do, okay?"

"Okay, don't be a stranger, promise." The familiar timbre of his voice was so soothing, so good, I let him slither right back in.

"I promise."

So absorbed in my own thoughts, I was up the porch steps and had my keys in the lock before I realized Tobias had dropped my hand.

He had stopped on the penultimate step and for the first time in our lives we were almost face-to-face at eye level.

I looked around us, trying to determine if something had caught his attention that I also needed to be aware of. But the street was quiet and still as per usual, except for the loud cicadas.

"Hey, what's up?"

He was staring at me with a deep furrow between his brows.

"Are you okay?" he asked.

Answering a question with a question. This couldn't be a good sign. I pulled my key out of the doorknob and turned to face him more squarely.

"Yeah, why wouldn't I be?"

His mouth twitched, like he was chewing the inside of his cheek. Maybe he was rethinking whatever he was about to say.

"You've been distant, ever since the wedding."

Ah, yes. The infamous wedding. Sandra's comment had set me thinking and finally I could hold back the curiosity no longer.

Now that Emory and I were mutuals on Instagram, it had been absurdly easy to find a picture of her. Emory was not a prolific poster, so I didn't even have to scroll back very far to find a couple's picture of her and Tobias with different people. The girl he had his arm slung around must have been the ex. A petite brunette, she was almost comically small compared to him. Average pretty, but she was skinny so all the average dudes would consider her a hottie.

I now knew what his mother saw when she looked at me.

I shrugged. "I'm fine."

"Why do you do that? Why do you treat me like I'm some dumb troglodyte who doesn't know what an emotion is? You've done that our entire relationship."

"Relationship? What relationship?"

By the shocked look on Tobias's face, I imagine that came out harsher than I meant it to. It was kind of an honest question. I didn't refer to him as my boyfriend, and, as far as I was aware, he wasn't referring to me as his girlfriend. We had never had that specific conversation about exclusivity.

"Is that what this is about? Dammit, Bryn, do you need to hear me call you my girlfriend? I told you I only date one person at a time."

"Yes, but—"

"But what?"

"I don't believe this is real." I flopped my arms helplessly. There. There it was. Words put to the gnawing feeling that had been present in the back of my mind since the day we met.

His eyes widened. "What does that mean?"

"You. Us. I don't believe we are real."

He blinked, like he really had no idea what was going on. "What are you talking about?"

"I saw her, Tobias! Your ex."

"She has nothing to do with this."

"She has *everything* to do with this."

"How?"

Was he really going to make me spell out every detail? "We don't exactly have a lot in common."

His frown deepened. "Are you saying...I can only date short girls with brown hair?"

"You know what I mean."

He crossed his arms, obstinate. "No, I don't. Explain it to me."

"I'm not exactly...like other girls. A lot of other girls. I'm above average...in a lot of ways." I gestured vaguely to the spread of my hips. For some reason, I was without words to describe what I wanted him to see. Like, if I put words to it, somehow, finally, Tobias would see what everyone else saw. And that would shatter me into a million pieces.

His gaze flicked down my body, but it was clinical, detached, and missing the heat I was accustomed to seeing and feeling.

"Have I ever, once, made you feel like I didn't like you just the way you are? Once?" His tone was inflectionless and I knew I had broken the fragile thing that had been growing between us.

I didn't have anything to say, because my answer was no. And yet and yet. The feeling was there. That I couldn't trust my own judgement.

I shook my head, throat tight.

"Then what? What happened to make you pull away so hard?" I fiddled with the ruching on the front of my dress, anything to keep my hands busy and my eyes away from his. "Bryn, you have to say something."

"Your mom"—I swallowed hard—"said something, to me at the wedding." I still couldn't bring myself to say the elusive F word. Not to him.

"Did she hate you? My mom hates everyone."

I could have laughed; his response was almost identical to Emory's. I wanted to laugh to diffuse the tension that hung so heavy in the air, to rewind the last few minutes that had passed between us, but Tobias's face was still set in a frown, a hard line between his brows.

"Yeah, but she's your mom."

"And? She doesn't get a vote in who I date." He had a counter for everything. But, of course he did, because Tobias was perfect and I was decidedly...not.

"You say that now." They all did. Until it was time to start introducing you to their friends, until it was time for an event and you didn't fit the part. Until it was time to lose your virginity in a school locker room and he wouldn't even *look* at you after when there were other people around.

I choked on a sob and Tobias's face immediately softened and he reached for me, always the white knight. But this time, I took a step back.

"Tobias...I-I can't. I can't do this." My voice was strangled, raw.

He let out a huge sigh, eyes flicking away into the darkness. His hands rubbed absently down his shirt and into his pockets. He straightened and I knew he was going to leave. He was going to walk away. And it was irrefutably my fault. The knot in my throat tightened.

"I'm sorry that someone hurt you. But I can't fix you and I can't save you." His body turned away from me. "Oh, and I thought you might want to see this. You missed it earlier, when you went outside to do, whatever." He'd pulled a neatly folded piece of paper out of his pocket and held it out towards me between two fingers, like he was handing me a business card.

My hands trembled but I couldn't force myself to reach out and take whatever he was offering. I was utterly terrified of what it could be.

He waited for half a breath before leaning down and setting it on the porch.

And then he was gone.

When I could breathe again, I picked up the piece of paper, unfolded it, read the title was "Green Haired Girl," and promptly buried it in my purse.

He had written a poem about me.

A fucking poem. And read it to a room full of fucking people. And I was too much of a coward to read anything past the title.

Amera's weird look and abrupt exit to hang out with Elliot suddenly made a whole hell of a lot more sense.

I managed to make it into the house and into my room before breaking down completely. And it was only one ragged and desperate cry into my pillow. I couldn't even cry appropriately for him, that's how fucked up I was.

I sent a quick text to Sheenah.

I need to come home.

I had failed as Vivien. I had failed as Bryn. I didn't know who else—or what else—to be.

CHAPTER TWENTY-TWO

SURPRISE, BITCH

Sheenah, bless her heart, was able to clear her schedule for me for the next weekend.

So I only had to make it through one week of pure hell.

And by pure hell, I meant waiting to hear from Tobias but knowing he would probably die before texting me. I had used up all his gentlemanly goodwill.

He'd even unfollowed me on Instagram and gone private, which fucking stung. He might have even done that that night, but I had made myself wait at least twenty-four hours before checking. I wanted to see if he had posted anything vague and sappy, but I knew he was too good for that.

I wanted to post something vague and sappy, but without him following me anymore, that was kind of pointless. Besides, I didn't really relish the idea of thousands of followers knowing my five-month nonrelationship had already crashed and burned.

On Tuesday morning, I spent the entire two hours of Advanced Advertising scrolling through pictures of us on my phone.

On Tuesday afternoon, I spent Social Media Campaigns catching up on The Wrong Swipe questions, fixing other people's problems so I didn't have to spend the time thinking about my own.

On Thursday morning, I mindlessly stared at the front of the room in Advanced Advertising, pretending I was being attentive. In silence. That drew the attention of some of my classmates, because I was not the quiet girl in class.

On Thursday afternoon, I spent Social Media Campaigns stalking the various social medias of anyone remotely connected to Tobias, in the hopes of stumbling upon any information he might have shared. What, exactly, I hoped to find was beyond me. I also spent part of that time drafting texts I would never send in my Notes app.

I'm sorry I'm sorry I'm sorry
Sorry didn't feel like enough.

By the time Friday rolled around, I was too indifferent and emotionally numb to sit through my senior seminar Lit class, so I skipped it. Emotionally numb, just the way I liked it.

Amera leaned in the doorframe to my room and watched me pack a weekender.

"I know something happened, but you won't talk about it."

"Right. I won't talk about it." I shoved clothes into the bag with more force than completely necessary.

She continued, "So I can't really give you tailored advice, since I don't know all the details. But are you sure you want to do this?"

With a forearm, I scooped a dresser-top full of toiletries into the bag and zipped it. Slinging the handle over my shoulder, I turned and faced her.

"I'm just going home for the weekend, Amera."

Her brows had that *I don't believe you* tilt to them. "Seeing anyone I should know about?"

"Nope."

I moved to walk past her, but she grabbed my hand. "I know being all surly and stoic and shit is your brand, but you don't have to carry this alone."

It dawned on me that, almost four years later, I was still holding Amera at arm's length, still couldn't let her all the way in. And she knew it like Tobias knew it.

My shoulders sagged in a way I hadn't felt in years. I inhaled. I squeezed her hand. "I know. Later, okay? I'll tell you later."

"Just don't do anything you'll regret."

I scraped out a laugh. "Where were you a week ago?"

As a college student without a vehicle, I learned very quickly during freshman year who the other kids from my hometown were and whether or not they had access to vehicles. It was easy enough to find out if Darah was going home for the weekend and would welcome a little extra gas money.

The funny thing about the whole ride home song and dance is that I had a fully paid for, fully insured car sitting in my mother's garage. She let me use it on the rare occasions I needed it when I was home, but wouldn't let me take it to school because "walking would do me good."

Joke's on her because I figured out the bus system my first week.

I had Darah drop me off at a local dive to kill some time. Sheenah wasn't able to meet until almost eight and I was not hanging out with my mom that long. I'd go over there just long enough to drop off most of my stuff and then meet Sheenah.

I posted up in a corner booth and ordered a chocolate milkshake.

The waitress who brought out my milkshake was a girl I'd gone to high school with but didn't really know.

She set the glass down on the table and cocked a hip. "Vivien Leigh. Don't see you around here much."

The small talk took me aback. I honestly hadn't expected her to remember my name. She was wearing jeans, an apron, and a branded T-shirt, her brown curls short and flouncy.

"Oh, hi, Jenna. Yeah, I'm at school, mostly."

She beamed. "Good for you. I always knew you were going places."

I snorted. I'm not sure I'd agree with her, but I doubted she was ready to hear about the various ways my life was currently in shambles.

She didn't seem to notice the noise I made. "You're hanging out with Sheenah later, right?"

My eyebrows rose. "Yeah...how did you know?"

"She told me y'all were still pretty close. So, hey, I might see you later, right? Sheenah was going to come to a party with a few of us."

Sheenah had failed to mention that to me yet. "Yeah, sure."

"Great! See ya later!" And then she sashayed away to check on her other tables.

Well, that was weird. But random run-ins with people you went to high school with tended to be on this side of weird.

Sipping on my milkshake, I texted Sheenah.

So, uh, party later????

Yeah, sry, didn't know if you would want to go or not

Who told you?? Lol

Jenna at the diner

Ah

She's cool

Hope you don't mind

No, party sounds like what I need

There was nothing I loved more than putting booze on a broken heart. I just hoped I had managed to pack a party outfit.

It was only a ten-minute Uber ride to my mom's house that cost me ten dollars.

The sprawling Colonial with its immaculate landscaping, white façade, white columns, and white picket fence also put some kind of feeling in the pit of my stomach. I think it was dread. I hated coming back to the house where my dad died. It was cold. The interior was even worse. Straight out of a polished and perfect magazine, the only room that actually looked like real people lived there was mine.

The porch lights flickered on and I realized my mom had either heard the Uber pull away or noticed me standing idly in the driveway.

I straightened my spine and walked in, prepared to face whatever was waiting for me inside.

My mom was in the kitchen, a glass of white wine in hand. She was still in her usual work outfit.

She was the VP of Marketing for a large fried chicken chain, which was horribly ironic considering she never ate fried chicken. So she was always in some kind of branded top, straight pencil skirt, and matching sky-high stilettos, with her long hair pulled up into a tight bun. She was slender, but also rounded in all the appropriate places, thanks to a steady regimen of Pilates, yoga, barre, and whatever else was on her gym's menu.

It honestly looked exhausting being that tight-laced and strapped up.

I used to think her job was cool, back when she was just a marketing associate, and even cooler that she got to bring home so much branded swag.

But then I wore one of the shirts to school and this little asshole named Cameron said I was the perfect mascot for fried chicken since I must eat it so much to be so fat.

And there ended my wearing of branded shirts and enthusiasm for my mom's career.

Sipping her wine, she gave me a look that said she disapproved of literally everything about me. "Vivien. You should have called or texted. I know you're on that phone all day."

I chewed on the inside of my cheek to prevent the quick escape of a smart-ass comment. It was two nights. We could be amenable for two damn nights. I had been actively trying to stay off my phone today because the urge to text Tobias was so strong my fingers practically itched with it.

SOMETIMES LOVE AIN'T ENOUGH

"Sorry, Mom." An apology with no qualifiers was usually the best way to go to appease her. "It's only a couple nights. I'll stay out of your way."

She swirled the glass. "What are your plans?"

"Sheenah's picking me up in a few. I've gotta go change." I scurried away before she could say anything else.

I didn't dawdle getting dressed. Mostly because I hated being back in the time capsule that was my childhood bedroom and all the memories there, but also because an incoming text from Sheenah said five minutes. There wasn't time for a lot of hair and makeup, so I just brushed my hair up into a fluffy high pony and threw on my lashes and a copious amount of eyeliner.

My mom was still in the kitchen when I walked back out, only this time she had discarded her heels and leaned against the quartz countertops.

Her eyes widened noticeably when she saw me. "Is that what you're wearing?"

I was wearing a gauzy maxi skirt and quarter-sleeve crop top. Honestly it wasn't even that revealing, if you didn't count the giant cutout over my chest. The skirt and top practically touched in the middle, but it was still two pieces anyway, and my mom didn't believe girls of a certain size should wear crop tops.

I swished the skirt innocently. "What's wrong with it?"

I knew what was wrong with it, but I liked to make her say it anyway.

"It's a little inappropriate for the public, don't you think?" she asked, like I was going to a board meeting.

"Everybody wears crop tops, Mom."

Her lips thinned in a straight line. "You shouldn't flaunt—"

"Flaunt what, Mom? What am I flaunting? You can say fat. It won't kill you."

She pushed off the counter. "You know I'm just thinking about what's best for you and what people will think of you."

"Maybe you should care more about what I think of you, instead of what people think of me."

And then I walked out because I saw Sheenah pull up into the driveway. So much for being amenable.

Sheenah drove a beat-up, manual, 90s Honda that made us both look gigantic inside. Standing together, we looked like the number ten.

Every inch six feet, she was built like an athlete but didn't play any sports, much to the chagrin of the girls' basketball and track coaches who had tried to recruit her in high school. She didn't have the time or tolerance for anything except her designs. She had a full ride to Penn Warren—we were supposed to room together—but backed out at the last minute, cancelled her housing, and switched her enrollment to a local community college.

She said she hadn't wanted to go that far away from her family, but I never did believe that was the whole story, especially since she ended up estranged from them at the end of that year. We both had always wanted nothing more than to get away from this town.

"Ooh, is that one of mine?"

I smoothed out the skirt that had hiked up when I got in the car. "Of course. A Sheenah original."

"I have some other pieces I'd like to fit for you. Maybe tomorrow, if you're game."

"You know I always am. How's your portfolio coming?"

Sheenah had done two years at the community college and was finishing her last two years at a Penn Warren satellite campus, but had her eye on a super elite design school.

"If you come over tomorrow for fittings, I'll be almost done." She gave me a side-eye.

"Girl, you know I will. Rain or shine. Hangover or no hangover."

"Oh!" she squeaked. "That reminds me. I brought something for you."

I grabbed the oh-shit handle as she relinquished control of the steering wheel to her knees in order to rummage around in the back seat.

Her arm reappeared with a bottle of Mountain Dew. "Mixed drinks!"

I gagged reflexively. The last time we mixed vodka and Mountain Dew didn't end well. Sheenah tossed it in my lap. "It's a diet."

"Oh, God, that's even worse." I took a sip of the foul mixture anyway because what the hell. "Are you drinking?"

"Tonight I'm just driving my sad friend around." She shifted gears and hit the gas to pass up a crawling SUV.

I took an unfortunately large swig of the drink and grimaced. I had already given her most of the story. "I think I really fucked up this time, Shee."

"He still hasn't texted?"

I shook my head.

"What a douche canoe."

I knew she was on my side because she was my best friend and that's what best friends do.

"I don't really think he's a douche canoe," I said quietly, almost despondently.

"Oh, honey."

I didn't want to dwell on the intonation in her voice. It said more than she did. So I changed the subject.

"So, where is this party and will we be there soon? And you're hanging out with Jenna now?"

"Whoa, one at a time."

She ticked off her answers on the steering wheel. "One, you left me so I had to find other people to hang out with sometimes. Two, it's Jenna's friend's cousin's party. And...what was the other question?"

I laughed and took another swig of the drink. "Are we almost there yet?"

Just as I said it, we turned onto a narrow street where one of the houses was surrounded by parked cars.

"We're here!"

"I gathered that."

With an impressive configuration of the gear shift, Sheenah swung her car in between two bigger sedans.

I left the diet Mountain Dew and vodka monstrosity in the car, because my stomach was already roiling and I didn't really feel like throwing up in Sheenah's car tonight.

I looped my arm through hers as we walked up to the house, which was suspiciously quiet for a party.

"Sheenah," I hissed, when we got inside.

It was less a "party" and more a "large gathering of people engaged in different activities at the same time." With pot. I caught a whiff of the distinct aroma as we passed a group of people playing

World of Warcraft on the large screen TV. Another group was having a heated argument over a game of Settlers of Catan.

I squeezed her arm. "Where have you brought me?"

"It's chill, right?"

Chill was one word to describe it. All the lights were on. I could barely hear any music and what I could hear sounded slow and mellow.

No one really paid us any attention until Jenna found us. She was wearing the same outfit from the diner and suddenly I felt extremely overdressed. Sheenah was cute in a casual and slouchy jumpsuit that had her logo stitched into the back.

"Sheenah! Vivien! Glad you could make it!"

She threw an arm around each of our necks. Her hair smelled like weed and strawberries. I was going to have to shower or stay over at Sheenah's tonight because I'm pretty sure there'd be a murder if I showed up back home smelling like weed.

"Thanks for the invite!" Sheenah said. I still had a hold of her arm because I was not letting her out of my sight in here.

Jenna pulled back and clapped her hands together. "So. What do you all want to do? I was just about to start a game of Monopoly, if you want in."

I was suddenly regretting my decision to leave the vodka in the car.

We ended up in a room that I think was supposed to be the formal dining room, but had been transformed into some kind of bohemian sitting room where a hipster white boy was strumming—badly—on a guitar.

I tried to sit down on a vacant bean bag, missed the middle, rolled off, pretended it didn't happen and that I had meant to sit down half-assed all along. Sheenah managed to hit the beanbag and propped her shoulder against mine.

I lasted all of two seconds before my phone came out and I started testing light and filters on Instagram. I needed to post some kind of picture showing what a great time I was having, in case Tobias was checking, even if he wasn't actively following.

The moody light in the room was actually pretty awesome.

I roped Sheenah into taking a few selfies with me.

I was finishing up my post and accompanying stories when I heard a familiar deep laugh that made my blood run cold. Sheenah must have heard it too because her eyes widened with alarm.

I whipped my head around just in time to see Justin Hershaw walk past the doorway, holding hands with a short, dark-haired girl I knew as Bekah.

"Fuck." I swiveled back to Sheenah. "What the fuck is he doing here?"

Sheenah shook her head helplessly, two-toned braids swinging. "I don't know. I didn't think he knew this crowd. Maybe Bekah does?" she added, as if that would somehow make it better.

This is not what this night was supposed to be about. It wasn't supposed to be about him. It was supposed to be about me, hanging out with my best friend, having a little booze, a good time, and forgetting about the guy I left at school.

Something burned inside me and I think it might have been rage.

After everything he said. After everything he told me. To show up here, with her.

I could feel the rage burning away the emotional numbness I'd felt all week, like flame to a candlewick.

I got to my feet with surprising agility. I heard Sheenah whisper my name, but it was too late. I found them in the kitchen with a group of people making drinks. So there was some alcohol in this house.

"Shaw," I clipped.

He flinched, my voice like the crack of a whip.

Surprise, bitch.

"I need to talk to you. Alone."

I avoided looking at Bekah, but she probably didn't have any idea what was going on. She was several years younger than us and I'm not even sure she knew who I was. Knowing Justin the way I did, I doubt he ever said anything to her about me.

She was short, slender, plain-faced, the curtain of her dark hair framing a pale, smooth face. She wore a T-shirt, jeans, and strappy sandals. She was wholly unremarkable. She had small teeth. The urge to hate her was strong, and I resisted it the best I could. She was not at fault here, as much as I would like her to be. And, technically, I was the Other Woman in this scenario, much as I had always been. I avoided flicking my gaze to her stomach, which was still perfectly flat.

He regained his composure quickly and shrugged, following me from the kitchen.

I entered the first empty room that I found, which just happened to be someone's bedroom. Previously, the knowledge of Justin following me into a bedroom would have sent my heart and head into a tailspin, but I couldn't feel anything over the rage pounding in my ears.

I whirled on him as soon as I heard the door close.

"What's up, Vivien?"

He just stood there in a stupid T-shirt and stupid basketball shorts, his gaze landing on literally everything except me.

"Are you fucking kidding me right now? After all that bullshit you laid on last week? After you practically begged me to answer the phone?"

He didn't even have the courtesy to look sheepish, just mildly uncomfortable.

"Are you going to say anything?"

"What do you want me to say? She's having my baby."

"Last week you weren't sure."

"Yeah, well."

Yeah. Well. What the hell was that supposed to mean? I didn't have enough lucid brain cells to riddle it out. I was just desperate. Desperate for something to bring him back to me.

"I've loved you since I was fifteen years old."

That got his attention. He finally looked at me and cocked his head. "Why?"

Of all the things he could have said, that was not what I expected.

I deflated like a popped balloon, the boiling rage melting away to be replaced by something else.

Why, indeed.

Because he was my first and we continued having mediocre sex? Because he said all the right things and was conventionally attractive and that made me feel good? Because he was a bad boy and if I only tried hard enough, loved hard enough, I could change him into something better?

Is that all I deserved? Years of mediocre sex and the scraps of his attention when he felt like giving it?

A thought hovered at the edge of my consciousness. A truth I'd known for a while now but was too afraid to admit, even to myself. To let it be thought, to let it be acknowledged, was a bell that could not be unrung.

Because you're afraid no one else will ever love you.

I pressed both hands to my abdomen to remind myself to breathe.

There it was.

That parasitic, insidious thought. Why I always boomeranged back to Justin. If he was always there, if I always had him, if he always had a piece of me, I couldn't be fully available for anyone else. And I couldn't get hurt.

But that wasn't true, because I was fucking hurt.

I was hurt by Justin, constantly. I'd let him do this to me, rip away little pieces of me bit by bit, until I was not someone I recognized. Not someone I wanted to be.

The desperate girl who cornered the boy who had never loved her in some random person's bedroom while his pregnant girlfriend waited outside.

I deserved more.

I deserved to be whole.

I deserved to have poems written about me and read to a room full of people.

I deserved to be loved in the light.

I inhaled a deep breath. "I wish you and Bekah the best."

I moved to walk past him, but he grabbed my wrist, the flesh of his palm like a brand on my skin.

"Vivi, wait—"

I jerked free and gave him a look that I hoped withered his balls. "Please don't contact me again."

After showering and spraying my clothes down with a fragrance mist, I did something I should have done years ago. I deleted his contact from my phone and blocked him on all my social media.

I texted Tobias.

I fucked up. I'm sorry.

Then I turned my phone off and chucked it across the room. I didn't want to be able to hear it chime with any notifications, or, worse, not chime at all.

I burrowed into the overly plush comforter of my childhood and finally, finally broke down in the way I wanted to on the night Tobias said goodbye.

Chapter Twenty-Three

ICON OF FEMALE RAGE

It turned out crying my brains out wasn't the best idea because I looked like shit in Sheenah's mirror.

Sheenah had turned her small studio apartment into a workroom. Her bed was shoved haphazardly into one corner, while the rest of the space was stuffed with racks of fabric, dress forms, half-made outfits, and her sewing machine.

I had picked up McDonald's sweet teas for us on the way over as a delicious pick-me-up, but the sugar did nothing for the huge bags under my eyes and swollen lids.

I usually enjoyed this part of the process, but having to stare at my bloated face for hours in the mirror—and be reminded of why it was so wrecked in the first place—was pure torture.

Sheenah sucked on her straw, head tilted, thin, round glasses perched on the tip of her nose as she surveyed her handiwork. The red portion of her hair was piled on top of her head in a messy bun, while the platinum-blonde underside spewed over her shoulders.

The dress she had on me was actually supposed to be a couture gown, even though it wasn't quite there yet. The underdress was a super structured corset that had my boobs almost up to my chin with an attached long organza skirt.

Sheenah started one-handedly draping more organza over my body, playing with the shape and the idea of gauzy sleeves.

"What do you think?"

"Well, I can't really breathe."

She chewed her straw as she sat back down. "Yeah, the cleavage is a little...intense. I can fix that!" She jotted down a note in the little notebook propped on her knee.

"Don't get me wrong, I'm all about intense cleavage. I would say this cleavage is more...destructive."

She laughed. "Noted. Intense, not destructive." Her pencil scritched across the page as she made a quick sketch. "What do you think about sleeves?"

I turned my shoulders in the mirror, ran my hands down the velvet boning. "What about one sleeve? Like, here?" I gestured to the middle of my bicep.

She stared at me for a minute with her mouth slightly open. "Genius."

Setting down her sweet tea, because apparently she needed both hands now, she turned to a fresh page in her sketchbook and began sketching furiously. She spent several minutes sketching and muttering under her breath.

"This is why you're my best friend," she said finally. She stood up and pulled the extra fabric off my left shoulder and started pinning some of it to my hip. "Are we thinking of a dramatic train or side slit? Or both?"

I met her eyes in the mirror and we said simultaneously, "Both."

She laughed. "God, I love that movie."

I smiled, but my stomach clenched with uncertainty. Being with Sheenah always brought back fond memories, like two outcast girls huddled in the dark eating popcorn and watching *The Road to El Dorado* obsessively. Why were we obsessed with *The Road to El Dorado*? Who knew. Maybe she was the Tulio to my Miguel. It was just one of our many things.

Thinking back to that girl made me uncomfortable because I thought she was long gone. I had worked so hard to become someone, something different. But with Sheenah, in this town, I fell back so easily into her shell.

I took a deep breath, forgetting what we were doing, and Sheenah squealed.

"Don't move!"

I froze. "Sorry!"

Chastised, I stood as still as humanly possible as she finished up her pinning.

"Okay"—she rubbed her hands together—"we can get you out now."

She carefully undid the dress from around my body and transferred it to a dress form—which I had also modeled for—while I put my slouchy clothes back on.

Grabbing my sweet tea, I took a seat on the floor. "It's going to be beautiful, SheeBee."

"I hope so. I'm planning on it being the crown jewel of my admission portfolio." She fluffed the fabric. "I'm thinking of calling it Medusa." Her gaze slid to me to test my reaction.

I tapped a finger against my chin. "Terrifying and beautiful. Turns men to stone. Icon of female rage. Sounds about right."

Sheenah finished adjusting Medusa and then came to sit cross-legged in front of me. "So, are we going to talk about what happened last night? Or no?"

Sheenah, angel that she was, did not pry as she drove me home, sobbing, last night. She knew all would be revealed when I was ready.

Was I ready, though?

Better now than letting it fester.

Sheenah listened, rapt, while I relayed the whole tale to her. It actually didn't take that long because the ending chapter of the Justin Hershaw saga was blessedly short.

When I finished, her liquid brown eyes were contemplative. She made that screeching sound with her straw against the plastic lid. From experience, I knew she was weighing her next words carefully.

"Give it to me. I can handle it," I said, with a resolve I didn't feel.

"Girl. Did you really tell him you loved him?"

I grimaced at the memory. It was almost all so surreal, like it had happened in a dream and not real life. Or that I had been a woman possessed. Which was quite possible. Possessed by a mad demon into doing and saying things I would never say under any other sane circumstance. But Justin had that effect on me and he always had.

"Hey, I'm really proud of you. Things might suck now, but you did the right thing."

My shoulders sagged. "Why does the right thing feel so damn bad?"

"It just does. That's the way it works."

I snorted. "That's the worst advice ever."

"I'm not the advice columnist."

I let out a primal sound, somewhere between groan and gurgle, and collapsed onto the floor. My friends loved using that one against me. Just because I could dish advice all day long, didn't mean I could actually take it. Obvi.

My arm was slung over my face, so the resulting, "I know," was muffled. Sheenah heard it anyway.

"I don't want to kick you when you're down or anything, but this was honestly a long time coming. Not to say I told you so or anything." She sucked smugly on her straw.

"I know," I said again. "There's something else."

Her eyebrows disappeared into her bangs. "Oh?"

"I texted Tobias. He hasn't responded." I tried not to sound so despondent about the whole situation.

"Well, that's okay."

"It is?"

She nodded once in the affirmative. "Do you want him back?"

"Yes."

My answer was immediate because I didn't have to think about it because I had been thinking about it since that night. Tobias wasn't just dreamy as fuck. He was kind and funny and thoughtful and I liked the person I was with him. If there was one thing I was sure of, it was that I wanted Tobias Doan back, no matter the cost to my ego or my pride or whatever else it was that had made me push him away. He was everything I had ever dared to dream of...everything society told me I'd never have.

"Then get him back."

When I got back home, Mom was in the living room sweating to some strange yoga-Jazzercise hybrid in her designer spandex.

I said a quick, "Hey, Mom," and made a beeline for the stairs that would take me to the safety of my room.

"Vivien." She paused her video and wiped the two droplets of sweat off her smooth forehead. "How's Sheenah?"

"She's good."

She'd finally turned around and her eyes immediately landed on the McDonald's cup in my hand. Thus, the reason I wanted to scurry away to my room as fast as possible. Her lips thinned.

"I didn't eat anything. It's just tea."

"You know sugary drinks are just wasted calories. They don't provide any nutritional value. I made green smoothies." She pointed to the side table, where her half-full glass of thick green goo waited.

I tried not to physically gag.

"I know about calories, Mom, because you always remind me."

It was a tale as old as time in our household when I was growing up. No sodas, no juice, no chocolate milk. If we just had to drink milk it had to be skim only. When I got sick, I might have a Sprite cut with so much water I'm not sure why she even bothered.

I wondered if she ever thought her militant rules and ever-growing list of criticisms had the opposite of their intended effect. But that would mean *she* failed instead of *me*.

"Well, I wouldn't have to remind you if you acted like you knew."

"What if I just don't give a fuck?"

The shock that registered on her face was impressive given the amount of Botox and fillers she's had.

"Vivien, what's gotten into you?"

It dawned on me. Just as I had accepted crumbs of affection from Justin all these years, I had done the same with my mom. And I was tired of starving.

"Guess what, Mom? I don't give a fuck about diets or calories or macronutrients or intermittent fasting or whatever else some charlatan on the internet is trying to sell you. It may come as a total surprise to you, but I actually like myself, fat ass and all. Oh, and other people actually like me too." I braced myself against the banister. "So now you get to decide if you can love your fat daughter...or not."

My heart was pounding so hard I could hear it in my ears.

I was halfway up the stairs when I heard her voice. "Vivien, wait."

I didn't want to stop. Didn't want to turn around and face the consequences of my words. But there was a tremor as she tripped over my name that was unfamiliar.

So, I stopped and looked.

I had been spending so much time around Tobias that everyone else looked small, but standing at the bottom of the stairs, fingers nervously playing with her small wrists, my mother looked especially tiny.

"Vivien...I...I." She swallowed. "I do love you." Her voice was barely a whisper. "How could you say that?"

A small tingle of regret had started to form in my chest, but the rage burned it away. "Really, Mom? You constantly criticize me and body shame me and I'm supposed to interpret that as love?"

Her mouth opened and I expected one of her familiar lines to come rolling out. The body shaming was for *my* benefit. But she closed her mouth, ran her palms down her pants, glanced off into the distance without a word. And then.

"I'm sorry."

That...was not what I was expecting. My shoulders slumped. I had been gearing up for a fight and she just...surrendered. Now I was well and truly out of my depth.

"Vivien, I'm sorry." She inhaled. "Go put your stuff away. I'll make lunch. How's chicken tetrazzini sound?" And then she disappeared into the kitchen.

I grabbed the railing so I wouldn't collapse on the stairs. Chicken tetrazzini used to be one of my favorite dishes before my mother decided big, creamy, cheesy pasta bakes had to be permanently banned.

Hell had definitely frozen over.

After the most awkward chicken tetrazzini lunch of my entire life, I was finally able to ensconce myself in my room. There was one more thing I needed to do.

I rescued Tobias's poem from the bowels of my purse and sat on my bed, gently spreading it out on my thigh and smoothing the creases from the paper with a forefinger.

The poem was handwritten, the letters tall, strong, and neat. There wasn't a mistake on the page, not one word erased or scratched out. Did he rewrite it endlessly, until it read the way he wanted? Or had it poured from him, perfect the first time?

I didn't think I had any tears left in me, but they came anyway, soft and silent as I read what he had written about me. What he had *proclaimed* about me.

The girl he had depicted on the page was, to put it mildly, a goddess. A Venus of Willendorf. An infinite enigma with malachite hair and dancing eyes. She was a collection of contradictions, hard and soft, curious and cautious, tender and vulnerable but impossibly impenetrable, suffering and rejoicing. A thunderbolt to the chest when we first met.

That was what Tobias saw when he looked at me.

Not a scarred girl crippled by her self-doubt and haunted by the relationship that never was.

Not a fat girl.

Tobias had declared every feeling he'd ever had about me to a room full of people while I had walked out.

Shit.

No wonder he hadn't answered my text message. It was woefully inadequate.

I inhaled sharply, swiping at my wet cheeks. My insecurities had been showing—had been for a while—and I needed to tuck them back in. They could only define me if I let them. I did not have to be the girl defined by her inability to let someone in, pushing people away before they had the chance to hurt her.

I took a picture of the poem and sent it Sheenah. Her reply was immediate.

GIRL. I really can't believe you right now.

I'm crying. He's so perf.

I know. Me too. And then I added some crying emojis for emphasis.

One of my favorite pieces of advice to dish out on The Wrong Swipe was to believe people when they showed you who they truly are. Because they always do, eventually.

Tobias had shown me who he really was and all I had to do now was believe him.

CHAPTER TWENTY-FOUR

NERUDA, HUH

It took almost a week of walking past King Hall and peeking in the door to catch Tanner at the desk.

I readjusted my crossbody, swiped my student ID, and walked in.

Tanner was smiling until he saw that it was me. His smile transformed into a deep frown and his eyes narrowed as I approached the desk.

"I was rooting for you, Bryn, I really was."

"I'm sorry."

I wasn't sure why I was apologizing to him, but it felt right. I also felt a small surge of hope knowing that Tobias obviously told Tanner what happened. He might not have been shitposting about me on social media, but he was talking about me to his friends.

"You did my boy dirty."

"I know. Listen"—I smacked my palms flat on the desk—"I need to know his schedule." Yes, we had been hanging out a lot, but we were only a couple months into the semester and I barely had my schedule memorized, much less Tobias's.

The look Tanner gave me was full of suspicion. "Why?"

"I'm going to get him back."

He hesitated for a second and then grinned. "You got a pen?"

I whipped out one of my favorite Sharpie pens from the pocket of my dress. "I'm a writer. I always have a pen."

"Oh," he said brightly. "That reminds me." He rummaged around behind the desk and came up with a glossy copy of the *Penn Warren University Ledger*, spring edition. Most of the ledger's content was all online these days, but we still put out a physical copy twice a year, filled with lots of extras you couldn't get on the website. Tanner thumbed through the ledger. "I'm still upset with you, but my girlfriend will murder me if I tell her I saw you again and didn't ask."

He finally found what he was looking for: the long article I researched and wrote about recognizing and preventing dating and relationship violence in college students.

"Wait. What's happening?"

He turned the ledger towards me, open to the title page of my article, where my headshot and bio were. "Sign please."

I almost laughed, but held it in. "You want an autograph?"

"My *girlfriend* wants an autograph. Signature first, and then you can have your intel."

I bit my lip to hold back my grin and did as he asked, flourishing a large, curlicue *B* over my face.

I blew on it to dry the Sharpie and slid it back to Tanner. "Done."

He put the ledger in the safety of his backpack. "Okay, listen up."

Triumphantly, I walked away with Tobias's desk schedule, class schedule, and as many details as Tanner knew about his extracurricular activities.

As soon as Tanner mentioned the open mic night, a light bulb went off in my head and I could have smacked myself. *Of course.*

Good thing it was Thursday.

I recruited Amera and Sebastian for moral support. Sebastian took a lot of convincing, but I wore him down with a lot of crying emojis.

"Are you sure this is a good idea?" Amera asked as I was getting ready.

"Yes. It has to be grand. Like, romcom movie grand."

I had on a low-cut, teal green floral maxi that almost matched the color of my hair. The dress made me feel good, which was what I needed the most. If I was about to make a fool of myself, I was damn sure going to look good doing it.

"What if he says no?"

I finished spritzing on my favorite perfume. "It doesn't matter," I said with more conviction than I felt. It *would* matter and I might not survive his rejection. The idea that Tobias was no longer interested was one that loomed large in my thoughts. Thoughts I tried my best to ignore so I could focus on enacting my plan.

Amera had helped me style my hair into one of those braid crowns, and I added a pair of dangly gold earrings that brushed my collarbones. I was an ethereal, sexy, flower queen, no matter what happened.

I repeated that mantra in my head as we made our way to the café. I had sent Bastian ahead to scope out the place and talk to the emcee. I didn't want Tobias to spot me before the right moment and ruin everything by taking off. I also needed him to actually be there. I wasn't about to lay myself bare more than once.

Amera came speed-walking back out to my hiding place behind a thick column, out of sight of the door or large windows of the café.

"Okay, Tobias is in there. I think we can get you in without him noticing, but he's definitely gonna notice when you get up on stage."

I nodded vigorously, not trusting myself to speak.

Amera's eyes widened. "Are you going to throw up? You're really pale. Well, paler than usual."

I shook my head. "No." I swallowed. "I can do this."

"I can just go get him, you know, and tell him to come out here."

"No." I stood up straighter and wiped my sweaty palms on my dress. "It has to be a grand gesture."

I swore I heard her mutter something about white girls under her breath, but she grabbed my arm and snuck me into the café anyway.

The emcee was actually a dude I knew from most of my advertising classes, so it wasn't hard to get bumped to the top of the list.

While he was making his usual intro, I hovered by the display case, trying not to pass out. I absolutely loathed public speaking with every fiber of my being. The fact that I was about to deliberately make myself the center of attention was anathema to my entire personality and upbringing. I preferred to be safely concealed behind my column and my computer screen.

I managed to spot Tobias's man bun right as David finished his bit.

"And now, gentle comrades, I have a very special treat for you tonight. Our first reader is none other than Penn Warren's Bryn St. Jean of The Wrong Swipe!"

There was more clapping and cheering than I expected. But, instead of making things better, that just made it worse. The ball in the pit of my stomach tightened. I gulped. If this didn't work, I would probably have to transfer schools for my final semester. Did they even let you do that?

David was smiling and waving me up and I felt Amera's fingers in my back, urging me into motion.

Oh, God, I was going to die.

I hitched on the biggest, fakest smile of my life—cheeks literally aching—and made my way to the small stage.

The microphone was already set to my height, which was great since I didn't know a damn thing about how microphones worked. One hurdle down.

I studiously avoided scanning the crowd for Tobias. I didn't want to meet his eyes or see any kind of expression on his face or I would definitely lose my nerve.

I focused on my phone and the screen pulled up to what I was going to read.

I cleared my throat and the microphone squealed. I felt my face heat. "Um, sorry y'all, first time." That got some chuckles. I cleared my throat again. "Okay, so, I did not write this, but I wanted to dedicate it tonight to someone very important to me. And to say sorry, because he won't text me back."

Some more laughs, some noises of outrage, and one familiar voice yelled, "Get it, bitch."

Bastian was at a table closest to the stage and had his arms up like he was at a concert.

A hysterical laugh almost bubbled up and out of me, but I managed to tamp it back down. I tapped my phone again because it had gone to sleep.

"Okay, here it goes."

I had pulled up my favorite translation of Neruda's Sonnet XVII, the one I had attempted to quote at him the day we met.

I cleared my throat again and started the poem, trying not to notice the slight waver in my voice.

I knew he would understand. Of all people, he would understand the most.

When I finished, I finally looked up for Tobias. The clapping was just a dull murmur in my ears as I scanned the crowd for him, for where I had last seen the back of his head, and couldn't find him.

He was gone.

He had *left*.

My public speaking nerves quickly curdled into dread.

He had left.

Before I could completely lose it on stage, David intervened.

"Thanks for that, Bryn, and good luck with your special someone. Wow! What a tribute!"

His hand on my shoulder helped me off the stage. It was a miracle I didn't just fall off and into a messy heap on the floor. I had just committed a very public act of self-flagellation and declaration of my feelings and he had just *left*.

I was going to fucking lose it.

That's when I finally noticed Amera at the back of the café, waving her hands and pointing towards the front door.

Oh, God, maybe he didn't leave.

For a brief moment, that felt worse.

I scurried towards the exit and burst through the doors into the autumn twilight.

He was just standing there, arms bursting out of a tight Catatonic Divinity T-shirt, hands tucked into the pockets of his painted-on blue jeans.

Why did he have to be so damn good-looking? My chest ached at the sight.

His face was schooled in neutrality, slate blue eyes contemplative and waiting. His whole demeanor and body language was calm and assured, in complete opposite to the messy and tangled feelings raging inside me.

"Neruda, huh," he said.

I could have exploded, just from the sound of his voice. I had missed him so much.

Say something, say anything.

"I'm sorry. Tobias, I'm so sorry. I didn't mean those things I said. I didn't mean to push you away. I—"

I snapped my mouth shut with a click of teeth. There were so many words that could follow that *I* and end with *you* and I wasn't sure which one of them was right. I needed more time. But I didn't have any more time.

"I want you, Tobias." I twisted my hands together. "I want you to be my boyfriend. Officially."

Old me would have cringed at this scene. But it was time to start being honest, with him and with myself.

He didn't immediately react to my declaration. Just watched me with those eyes. I'm pretty sure Amera and Sebastian were watching the show from inside the café and if Tobias didn't say something soon, I was going to melt into a puddle of embarrassment.

"Say something, please." My voice was hoarse with raw emotion. I needed to get off this emotional roller coaster I'd been on the last few weeks.

"You don't have anything to apologize for." He rubbed one of his hands across the back of his neck. "I pushed you too hard. I knew you were skittish and I pushed too hard. That's why I never asked you to be my girlfriend. I thought you would run off."

I stood with my mouth slightly gaping, stood in the knowledge that he was probably right. As much as I worried about exclusivity, I probably would have gone running in the other direction seeing how emotionally unavailable I was. I simultaneously wanted the relationship and feared it.

"Why didn't you answer my text?"

"I didn't know what to say."

"Are you serious?"

He shrugged and gestured towards the café. "I enjoyed the show, though." And then he grinned and it was the most beautiful thing I had ever seen.

I let out an exhale of breath. Men. They were all just dumbasses.

"Can we start over?"

He cocked an eyebrow. "How far over?"

I held out my hand. "Hi, I'm Vivien."

I had debated going by Vivien again since that night with Justin. Bryn was useful; I liked Bryn. But maybe she was too guarded, too distant. I wanted to reclaim my real name, take it back from Justin and give it to Tobias. Let Tobias see me, all of me, sharp edges and soft curves and scars and broken parts.

"Vivien," he purred, "is a beautiful name."

Then he took my hand in both of his and brought the back up to his lips. His beard rasped across my skin and my thighs clenched. How the fuck did I ever think this was not real?

He tugged me towards him, crushing my soft body flush with his hard one, fitting us together like a puzzle piece. His arms snaked around me, one hand brushing over the generous curve of my ass and the other sliding up my back. I was fully enveloped by his warmth and his scent.

I couldn't help but press my nose into his throat, to inhale that scent, sorely missed.

"Get a room!" Amera yelled and I could just imagine her hanging out of the café door, face contorted with glee.

Tobias laughed, the sound rumbling in his chest. He cupped my face, thumbs brushing over my lips.

"Vivien, will you go out with me?"

I sucked in air. "Um, let me think about—"

He shut me up with a rough kiss, which I returned in kind.

"If y'all have sex on this walkway, I'm filming it and putting it on the Internet!" That was Sebastian.

I disentangled myself from Tobias's arms reluctantly, but kept hold of one of his hands. "Where are you taking me this time, Mr. Doan?"

His lips quirked. "My room?" he said, hopefully.

I pretended to think about it. "Okay, but I get pasta after. Deal?"

He squeezed my hand. "Deal."

Epilogue

December

Dear Ms. Martin,

While we enjoyed meeting you and reading your application materials, we regret to inform you that you were not selected for this year's internship class. As you know, the program is very competitive and only accepts 1% of total applicants.

Please don't take this minor setback as a reflection on your work.

We look forward to hearing more from you in the future and wish you all the best.

Sincerely,

Dr. Mal Leeland, Director

School of Communications

As soon as the email had come in and I saw that it started with *while*, I knew it was going to be a rejection. Acceptance letters start with *congratulations!*

That knowledge didn't numb the sting, though. I imagined I lost out to some hard-hitting investigative journalists writing about corporate espionage and political corruption. Much like the divide between literary and genre fiction, the crevasse between investigative journalists and advice columnists was vast, although I believed we all were doing important work.

Pfft.

"One percent is really competitive."

Tobias's naked body was spread out over my naked body, so he could read the email over my shoulder. We were in his dorm room, the bright sunlight streaming in from the one window onto his plant babies.

"I know." I thumbed the rejection email into Trash so I didn't have to look at it mocking me anymore.

"Would it be a bad time to tell you I got an early decision for my first school and my safety school?"

I gaped. "Yes! Horrible timing!"

"You could apply to grad school. It's not too late."

Grad school wasn't on my plan B. What was my plan B anyway? I honestly hadn't given it a whole lot of thought, which was a mistake because now I needed it. I had been apparently living in a rich fantasy world in which there was no doubt I would get accepted for the internship.

"You could come with me?" Tobias said his words carefully, probably concerned with spooking me again with additional commitment. "You'll have to get a job, though, cause my graduate stipend is only going to be like 10k a year."

I laughed at that.

The idea of following a guy across state lines while he pursued his dreams set off alarm bells in the back of mind.

I was supposed to be following my dreams.

But I could write anywhere. Wasn't my goal to take The Wrong Swipe national? Maybe even work on compiling a book? I could do that literally anywhere. I just needed to talk to my editor about rights and such. And a bigger city would mean more opportunities. Maybe a robust writing community. Networking. I didn't need the internship to accomplish my goals. Would have been a nice boost, but I could still do it.

"Are you thinking about it? Because you look like you're thinking about it."

"I'm thinking about it."

After graduation, there wouldn't be much left for me here. What was I going to do, really? Move back home with my mother? I wouldn't have previously considered that as a viable option, but she hadn't uttered a word about diets or weight since our confrontation. We danced delicately around the subject—it had been our sole conversation topic for so long. But she was trying. I would miss Amera and Sebastian, but Amera would have her choice of jobs after graduation and Sebastian was going to be a fifth-year senior.

Sheenah would need me for a final fitting and photographing for Medusa, but once that was finished? Why not? A new city could be my big break. Chicago or Seattle.

I drummed my fingers on the bed. "Okay, but I'll need to do some research on which city would be best."

His eyes sparkled. "Oh, so now you're choosing for me?"

"I just want to provide some additional information for you to make the right choice."

He laughed, then kissed the tip of my nose.

"Whatever. You know you love me."

"I do," he said, without a hint of hesitation or humor.

My chest tightened, almost as if I had suddenly stopped breathing. My limbs felt lighter, but I was still acutely aware of all the searing places Tobias's body touched mine. I exhaled. "Seriously?"

"And I know you love me because this is like the third time you've said it."

"That was an accident." I was surprised that he remembered my slipup at the wedding. After everything that happened, that night felt like a lifetime ago.

"Once is an accident. Twice is a pattern." He ran his hand through my mess of hair. "I love you, Vivien."

I laid my head down, cheek pressing into his warm forearm. "I love you, too, Tobias Doan."

Afterword

Thank you for reading *Sometimes Love Ain't Enough*!

Reviews are a great way to support authors, and I would appreciate you leaving one on a retail site or anywhere else on the internet. If you post about the book on social media, you can use the hashtags #sometimesloveaintenough or #slae so I can find, like, and share the post!

Be sure you're following me for updates about the next Penn Warren book, *What Kind of Fool*.

xoxo

jessica

About the Author

J.L. Minyard is the not-so-secret pen name of award-winning young adult author Jessica Minyard. Jessica is an author, poet, ISTJ, Sagittarius, and boy mom who lives and writes from the bluegrass.

For exclusive content, freebies, sneak peeks, and other updates, sign up for her newsletter: https://www.subscribepage.com/jessicaminyard

Follow her on social media:
Facebook: Author Jessica Minyard
Twitter: @callmeshashka
Instagram: callmeshashka

Sneak Peek

The following is an excerpt from the second book in the Penn Warren series, *What Kind of Fool*.

Please note that the text has not been edited and is subject to change in the final version, so please be gentle.

xoxo

jessica

What Kind of Fool

I was a cliché.

I stood there, hand on the gleaming silver steamer handle, remaking an angry white lady's drink because she swore I used coconut milk instead of almond.

I hadn't.

Five years as a barista and I knew how to making a fucking drink.

Couldn't tell Karen that, though.

So I remade it in stormy silence while my coworkers gave me knowing looks and I daydreamed about art school.

A fucking cliché.

I whipped back around and handed her the hot drink with a winning, well-practiced smile. She took it, a fake designer bag swinging on her arm.

We held eye contact while she tasted the drink, holding up the afternoon coffee break line.

"Much better!" She smacked her lips.

"Always happy to help!" I chirped in my customer service voice.

Alanna, the shift manager, sidled up to me, the copious amounts of gold bangles on her arms clinking merrily. "Incoming. Your favorite customer."

She breezed away while I scanned the line in a panic, barely registering the next customer's extensive deviations from the recipe, Sharpie scrawling down his cup. I finally spied him, a few people deep.

Colton.

A whitecollar dudebro who worked in one of the large office buildings in the same strip as the coffee shop. I was used to seeing a lot of nine-to-fivers once or even twice a day as they went about their business. They were our regulars and biggest customer base. Most of them were perfectly pleasant and respectful of our parasocial relationship of customer and barista.

Not Colton, though.

Colton was some hotshot financial something or another and didn't let anyone forget it. Sometimes he came in alone, and sometimes he came in with a herd of other dudebros who all dressed the same in loafers, khakis, polos, and a branded company jacket and ID lanyard.

He was currently twirling his lanyard around in the air, headless of other people around him. Part of me wished he'd smack someone with it so they'd smack him back. Hopefully.

Colton tipped and expected you to smile and laugh.

He had asked me out no less than five times and by the broad smile on his face as he approached the register, it seemed like today would be number six.

I'd hate to have to reject a guy six times.

I hitched on my work smile and held up my Sharpie and a cup.

"The usual?"

He put his hand on the counter top and leaned against it, coming as close to my face as possible before hitting the register. His cologne was an overwhelming, sharp musk that caused me to lean back.

"Sheenah, don't be like that." He grinned, in what I'm sure he thought was a charming way. And he might be attractive and charming to the right girl, but not me. He was too slick and sly and his eyes were cold.

"Like what, Colton? There's a line." I gestured, in case he couldn't see it.

"I have two tickets to the concert downtown tonight," he said, as if he couldn't hear me. "One for the prettiest barista around."

I was seven hours into a ten-hour shift, so I honestly doubted that. Unless sweaty hair, smudged mascara, and coffee grounds-under-unkempt-nails were Colton's thing. Which was highly suspect, considering his head-to-toe branded clothes and accessories.

"I don't like music." I deadpanned.

He blinked a few times, processing this new information. "Everyone likes music."

"Not me." I wrote his name on his cup, as if I couldn't hear him. "The usual, then?"

He sighed dramatically, but finally lifted up from the counter and I felt the knot in my chest loosen.

"Only if you draw me a pretty picture."

Someone had let slip that I was an artist and ever since I'd been in charge of drawing on the billboards and people's cups, if they asked nicely. I was happy to do it for customers I liked, but unfortunately

SOMETIMES LOVE AIN'T ENOUGH

Colton wasn't one of those and also unfortunately he asked for one every time.

My fingers clenched around the Sharpie. It took all my effort not to draw a tiny man on fire. Instead, I drew a standard pumpkin, since it was October, after all.

I did his standard pour and handed him the cup.

"What? No hearts?"

There was that grin again, the slick one, as he eyed my baggy black shirt, covered in splashes of milk and syrup. The way he just...lingered...made my stomach roil.

He tipped his cup at me.

"One day, Sheenah. One day, you'll say yes."

He finally walked away, but the sick, twisted feeling in my stomach stayed. I could feel the color draining from my face; the burn of bile rising up my throat. The Sharpie clattered to the counter as I dropped it.

Alanna's hand was on my shoulder and her soft touch brought me back to the present, back to my body that was only mine now.

"Sheenah, are you okay?"

I shook my head. "No, I need to go vomit."

It took almost ten minutes of me hugging the porcelain toilet before someone came to find me. I had my cheek pressed to the cool lid; I hadn't actually vomited. Just dry heaved into the toilet until the feeling passed. The handle jiggled, then I heard the key turn in the lock. Only Alanna had a key to the restrooms.

"Hey, Sheenah, are you okay?"

I nodded, still facedown.

"Colton's an idiot, but I didn't think he was really bothering you."

I heard the door snick shut and then Alanna crouched down into my line of vision.

Alanna was maybe twenty-five with sharp eyeliner and an English degree. She was the most popular manager because she always reminded us to take our breaks, rarely asked us to cover a shift, and was magnanimous with the bathroom key, to both employees and customers.

"Do you want me to call his boss?"

Alanna's offer was tempting, but I was already shaking my head. On the off chance Colton's boss would actually do anything—other than immediately tell Colton—the brief flicker of joy it would bring me was not worth the risk, that I was sure of. Colton hadn't done anything other than be nauseatingly obnoxious. I hadn't seen him after work, as he had failed to follow through with any of his threats to meet me after my shift, and he hadn't tried to make contact on any social media.

Alanna frowned. "Are you sure?"

"I'll handle it," I said.

I wouldn't poke a sleeping bear because I knew how that story ended.

Made in the USA
Columbia, SC
19 August 2023

21764873R00164